DOCTOR WHO
THE ARK

GW00585249

DOCTOR WHO
THE ARK

Based on the BBC television series by Paul Erickson by
arrangement with the British Broadcasting Corporation

PAUL ERICKSON

Number 114 in the
Doctor Who Library

TARGET

A TARGET BOOK
published by
the Paperback Division of
W.H. ALLEN & Co. PLC

A Target Book
Published in 1987
By the Paperback Division of
W.H. Allen & Co. PLC
44 Hill Street, London W1X 8LB

First published in Great Britain by
W.H. Allen & Co. PLC 1986

The BBC producer of *The Ark* was John Wiles
the director was Michael Imison

Printed and bound in Great Britain by
Anchor Brendon Limited, Tiptree, Essex

ISBN 0 426 20253 8

Contents

1

The Steel Sky

Jungle.

Lush foliage crowded in upon itself beneath the tall trees. Here and there, amid dark shadows cast by overhanging branches, small pools of light picked out brightly-coloured flora.

Shimmering mist hovered in patches over the dense tangles of undergrowth, thinning away in places to reveal small clearings.

Into the still air rose a murmur of activity from the teeming jungle floor, pierced by sharp cries which indicated the presence of larger forms of life.

Animals.

A mynah bird fluttered from branch to branch, its eyes picking out the familiar scene; other birds, some in flight, others resting ... and on the ground a lion padding from one copse to another, causing gazelles to scatter from its path in a flurry of alarm. A cacophony of chatter, and monkeys which had been picking at the kernels of fallen nuts scampered up trees to reach safety.

The lion having passed, the other animals re-emerged to feed upon the shrubbery. Zebras, kangaroos, tortoises and many other species mingled together in the ebb and flow of a densely packed animal kingdom.

Among them, reptiles.

So that a particular form of reptile life that moved among them passed unnoticed, obviously representing no threat.

But this creature was different from the snakes and lizards that were normally found in this jungle. In the first place it walked upright on two legs, two arms hanging at its sides. It made no sound, not even the hissing that other reptiles might make. And while its body was covered in scales, the head boasted a mop-like thatch of ginger hair.

Facially, it displayed three shrunken nostrils and a small, thin mouth from which a tongue occasionally flicked out.

But its most prominent feature was a large single eye that constantly swivelled as it looked around.

An eye that apparently accepted the scene as being normal. Having found it so, the creature moved on, disappearing into the shadows of the undergrowth.

No sooner had the creature disappeared than a different, alien sound was heard in the jungle. A whirring, mechanical noise that disturbed the sweltering, humid place ... and, as it echoed and then died away, the TARDIS police box materialised in the glade.

At first there was a startled and uncertain reaction from the crowded animals ... then, as silence returned, they resumed their business of foraging for food.

The door of the TARDIS opened and Dodo Chaplet emerged. An elfin-like teenager, she was dressed in the fashion of a page from the period of the Crusades.

She gazed around at the jungle that surrounded her and, in wonder, moved forward to touch the bark of a tree as though to make sure that it was real.

Finding that it was, she became conscious of the steamy, clinging heat of the place. And in response to it, she suddenly found her nose itching. Her fingers pinched at her nose, attempting to stifle a sneeze, but it came bursting forth.

'Atishoo!'

Dodo brushed her fingers across her nose and shook her head, seeking to clear it. Then she glanced up as Steven came out from the time-machine to join her.

He looked at her with barely concealed annoyance. 'And just where do you think you're going?'

'Out! I thought I'd get some fresh air!' Dodo replied defiantly.

'Nobody said you could go out!' Steven snapped.

'Do they have to, then?'

'Of course they do!' Steven shook his head in bewilderment at her recklessness. 'You don't know what you might have found out here. No gravity ... poisoned atmosphere ... all sorts of things.' Dodo started to move away from him. 'Look, stop tramping around over there ... What happens if you get lost?'

'In that case I catch a bus back!' came the answer.

'A *bus*!' Again Steven shook his head. 'What do you think you're talking about? I mean, just where do you think you are?'

'Ah! I bet you think you've caught me, don't you? I'll bet you think I don't know!'

'You do?' Steven asked.

'Of course I do!' Dodo replied with confidence.

'What ... this place? With all these strange animals ... and plants ... and things? You can't have been here before!'

'Yes, I have! I came here once with my school. It's called Whipsnade. It's just outside London.'

'Just outside ... now, wait a minute ...'

Dodo pointed away from the glade through the trees. 'I'll bet if you go down that path there you'll come to the American bison and the tea bar!'

Steven sighed in exasperation.

'We don't even know that we're on Earth,' he argued.

'Earth? *Earth?*' Dodo countered scornfully. 'This place couldn't be anywhere else, now could it?' She indicated. 'That's a chameleon ... and over there ... those are Malayan gazelles.' She peered at a bush. 'And on these leaves ... locusts.'

'How do you know all this?' Steven asked.

'Learned it at school. Natural history ...'

From the depths of the woods a baying howl echoed. Dodo jumped, losing something of her confidence.

Steven grinned. 'Having second thoughts?'

'No ... I just don't remember Whipsnade being so loud, that's all.'

*

Inside the TARDIS the Doctor pored over the instruments with a puzzled expression. He shook the Space Longitude Indicator, not quite believing its reading, but the figures that it spelled out remained steady. And it was the same with all the other instruments. However much he tapped and tweaked at them, the initial readings remained obstinately the same.

'Strange!' he muttered. 'Very strange.'

What was strange about them was the fact that they were *all* apparently working ... and *all* at the same time. And this really perplexed the Doctor, because it was indeed a rare day when something wasn't going wrong in his old war-horse, TARDIS. He could hardly remember the last time they had combined to give such consistent readings. He scratched his chin.

'Not since that trip to Venessia ... or was it Enlandia? That strange place where the one thing they didn't have was land. Nothing but water ... and that peculiar form of crystal ice.' He quivered, momentarily remembering the place well. It still gave him the shivers to think of it ... and remember the giant eels that had squirmed their way about the place.

But, no ... the readings were what they were ... and he glanced up when he heard the youngsters outside talking about the possibility of finding themselves on Earth.

The Doctor emerged from the TARDIS, shaking his head in bewilderment. He glanced at Dodo and Steven.

'Improbable as it may seem, the child Dorothea –'

'Dodo!' the teenager protested.

'Oh, yes, of course!' the Doctor conceded. 'I think Dodo may be right!'

Steven was puzzled. 'You mean ... it *is* Earth?' he asked.

The Doctor shook his head cautiously. 'I can't tell you just yet, not for certain. All I can say is that it is more likely to be Earth than anywhere else. But it is very strange, all the same.' He grasped the lapels of his jacket. 'You know, I've been taking a look at my instruments in there, and my readings are ... well, *very* strange!' Then he shrugged his shoulders as though finding a delight in a problem. 'Yes ... *very strange*

10

indeed.'

Elsewhere, activity was taking place in a control room.

A central panel was the obvious focus of all this activity. Monitor screens gave a constant display of everything that was going on, both within the Control Room and outside it. Fingers moved levers and the effect on the combined screens gave those within the Control Room a constant up-date on the information they required.

Those fingers belonged to humans ... and also to one-eyed, scaly reptilian creatures like the one who had wandered through the jungle earlier. They appeared to work and co-exist in harmony, humans and Monoids obviously having a common purpose.

One of the Monoids pressed the trigger of an information terminal. It whirred and passed out a sheet of paper. This was handed to one of the humans and passed along until it reached the hands of the Commander, a middle-aged man of erect stance. He glanced at the paper and frowned.

'Bring in the prisoner!' he demanded.

A door slid open and a young man was led into the Control Room by another man and a Monoid. The young man looked pale and apprehensive. He was brought face to face with the Commander, while other humans and Monoids studied him with detached curiosity.

'Niash,' the Commander addressed him, 'you have been found guilty as charged of the summons brought against you; that is to say, that you endangered our venture by failing to check the sealing valves properly.'

'Yes, Commander,' Niash admitted in an uncertain voice.

'By so doing you could have destroyed by an explosion everything that we ... and our friends, the Monoids ...' the Commander acknowledged the presence of the reptilians, who bowed respectfully '... will ever hope to achieve.' The Commander sighed. 'So now it is my duty to pass sentence upon you. According to Galactic Law, which I must administer, there are in these grave circumstances only two punishments: the one, expulsion into outer space; the other, miniaturisation. As you know, miniaturisation means you will be retained on micro-cell slides and be reconstituted in about seven hundred years from now when you will no longer be able to do any harm.'

Niash blanched. 'Death ... or suspended life?'

The Commander's voice was firm. 'Precisely! But it is up to you to choose, and before doing so you may consult with your defending counsel, Manyak.'

Niash nodded and turned to speak to the man who had helped escort him into the Control Room. While they conferred, the Monoid who had also assisted in the task stood silently by, apparently listening to their deliberations, his one eye swivelling as it watched their lips.

Mellium, a young girl, moved towards the Commander. 'Father, he only made one mistake. He won't do it again. You can't condemn him like this.'

'I have no wish to do so, but we are the Guardians of all life,' her father stated. 'It is the law, and it must be obeyed.' He indicated another young man. 'Zentos has made a sound case for the prosecution. The facts simply cannot be denied.'

Manyak and Niash had completed their quick consultation. Manyak turned to face the Commander.

'Niash accepts the sentence of miniaturisation and is grateful that you have not passed a harsher judgement.'

'Very well,' the Commander acknowledged. 'At least there is hope for him in the distant future.'

Turning to the others present, he announced: 'The sentence is confirmed. Let it be carried out.'

Niash was led towards a glass-fronted chamber. Mellium stepped forward and grasped his arm.

'I'm sorry, Niash,' she cried out. 'I wish there had been more that I could have done.'

Niash shook his head. 'The mistake was mine and the sentence is a just one. Now that it has finally been decided I am at peace with myself.' He smiled wryly. 'Sometime in the future I will remember you, but in the meantime, travel in hope.'

Her hands flew to her mouth, choking a sob, as she murmured 'Goodbye.' He stepped away from her and entered the chamber. A lever was pulled, there was a concentrated flash of light within the chamber and, even as the others watched, Niash grew smaller and smaller until finally he seemed to have been reduced to nothing. Then the bright light died down. Manyak opened the door of the chamber and stepped in to pick up the slide onto which Niash, now a mere speck, had been impregnated. Manyak placed it in a covering dish and carried it away out of the Control Room.

Zentos was conferring with a Monoid, not by speech, but by way of hand signals. The Monoid replied in kind and Zentos turned to face the Commander.

'My learned friend wishes to thank you, Commander, for the way in which you take care of us all.'

There was a general murmur of assent from all in the Control Room, both humans and Monoids. The Commander acknowledged this. Then, turning, he placed his hand on the shoulder of his still troubled daughter.

'It was the right thing ... the only thing ... to do, Mellium, if we are to succeed in our mission.'

Mellium nodded in resignation, finally recognising this to be true.

In the jungle the Doctor, Steven and Dodo were venturing a little further away from TARDIS, fascinated by their surroundings. The animals seemed to have accepted them, to the point they almost ignored them, but from among the trees a large beast moved in their direction.

Dodo was the first to see it and smiled as she pointed towards it. 'Oo ... look at him, then!'

It was a fully matured elephant which brushed the undergrowth with its trunk as it advanced. After a moment's hesitation they in turn moved forward to meet it and caressed its trunk and bowed head. Then, finding with its questing trunk that they had no food to offer, it moved on.

The Doctor stared after it and then at the jungle around them.

'Well,' he exclaimed. 'It's all very, very strange! That was an *Indian* elephant!'

'Yes, I know,' Steven responded. 'But what difference does that make?'

The Doctor chuckled. 'That's what I'm trying to work out, my dear boy!'

'Flowers from America, birds from Africa – and a whopping elephant from India,' Dodo ventured.

'Exactly, my dear,' the Doctor observed.

'It looks like specimens from all over the world.'

'Yes, you're quite right!' The Doctor nodded. Then he glanced up. 'Yes! And on top of everything else this is a jungle without a sky!'

Steven and Dodo glanced up.

'Hey, look at that then!' Dodo exclaimed.

'No sun, no clouds ... merely a metal roof!' the Doctor observed. 'But one that radiates some kind of light.'

Steven stared at the roof that spread as far as the eye could see. 'It's extraordinary!' he exclaimed.

The Doctor pursed his lips and glanced down at the ground. 'Yes ... but besides that there is something else ...'

'What's that?'

'The earth ... this soil we're standing on ... it appears to be trembling!' He stooped down and placed his hand on the surface. 'Yes! One can feel it!'

'Do you think it's an earthquake building up?' Steven asked.

'Or maybe more elephants ... or buffalo, or something ... charging!' Dodo ventured.

The Doctor shook his head. 'No! Nothing like those things you've suggested! The trembling would be intermittent. This is regular, without break, without pause. It's a machine of some kind. A mechanical vibration.'

'In what circumstances do you get things like this all coming together?' Steven asked. 'I mean, animals and plant life from all different continents?'

Dodo puffed out her cheeks and shook her head.

'And a metal roof and all this shaking?' she added. 'Weird!'

The Doctor had straightened up from examining the ground and held up his finger, glancing around.

'The answer could be quite simple! It could be ...'

'Yes?' Dodo and Steven asked in unison.

'... some kind of indoor nature park!'

They were amazed. 'On this scale?' Steven queried.

'Yes, improbable,' the Doctor rejoined. 'But possible!' He nodded his head, firming up his own belief. 'Definitely possible!'

'But are we on Earth or ...?' Dodo started to ask, but was unable to complete her question, as her nose suddenly became irritated again and she sneezed. *'Atishoo!'*

'H'm?' The Doctor glanced at her. 'Oh, bless you, my dear!'

'Thanks,' Dodo sniffed.

'But don't you have a handkerchief?' Dodo nodded. 'Then use it, my child. We must do something about that cold of yours.' The Doctor stared at her searchingly. 'That reminds me ... why are you dressed in those stupid clothes?' He indicated the Crusades period page's costume. 'Have you been raiding my wardrobe? Just what do you think you're doing? Re-enacting history? Returning to an age of heroism? Or playing charades!? H'm?'

'They suited me and I thought it was all right to wear them! Or do I have to ask permission for that, as well?' sulked Dodo.

'Oh, it's all right this time,' the Doctor replied with a wave of his hand. 'But you take care of them because you never know when you might need them again.' Having passed judgment on the subject he indicated their surroundings. 'But now we'll take a last look around and then we'll get you off to bed!'

'Does that mean ... *sniff* ... that you are going to send me home?'

'Oh, what a tempting idea! But I couldn't send you home if I wanted to!'

'All right then,' Dodo responded. She looked around with a mixture of curiosity and appreciation. 'I'm beginning to enjoy this space travel or whatever it is!'

With the Doctor leading the way, Dodo and Steven followed, moving deeper into the jungle.

But as they went it wasn't just the animals they had already seen and identified who watched them. For, from behind cover, a reptilian hand reached out and pulled aside the foliage in order to give a Monoid a better view of them. Its swivelling eye watched them for a moment. Then the creature drew back, heading off along another path.

The Commander checked the data that was being fed to him by the combined efforts of the humans and the Monoids.

'Everything seems to be going well,' he summarised, addressing Manyak. 'We are holding to the Main Edicts timetable.'

'Yes, Commander,' Manyak assented.

'The humidity levels in the jungle are normal,' the Commander's daughter, Mellium, concluded after checking several instruments. 'And that was our greatest concern.'

In the jungle the Doctor paused to mop his brow.

'No wonder that child has caught a cold,' he addressed Steven, indicating Dodo, who had run on ahead of them. 'The humidity in this place is somewhat oppressive, to say the least of it.'

'Just like being in a hot house,' Steven agreed.

'H'm? It reminds me more of the planet Sava. The last time I was there ...'

'When was that?'

'Oh, some time ago,' the Doctor rejoined cautiously.

Some time ago was right. No sense in telling the young man that it must have been three centuries in his terms, although in the Doctor's own knowledge such a time span had little meaning. Places were places, creatures were creatures . . . and time was time. All in the *now* period. That was the only way he ever experienced it, the only way he knew it.

His rambling thoughts were broken into by Steven suddenly calling out in alarm: 'Watch out, Dodo! Behind you!'

A tiger had emerged from the woods. It slunk forward . . . then charged at the startled Dodo.

The Doctor whipped off his jacket and waved it in the air as he and Steven hurried forward to her rescue. Instinctively they started shouting, trying to frighten the beast off . . . but then stopped suddenly in amazement as the tiger slowed down and, instead of attacking Dodo, started licking at her hand.

Dodo could hardly believe it. The tiger was full-grown, its fangs large and menacing, but the tongue that brushed over her hand was soft and warm.

She looked up as the Doctor and Steven approached.

'What do I do?' she asked, uncertainly.

The Doctor shrugged. 'Just try and stay calm, my dear. Don't make any quick moves.'

'That's all very well for you to say,' she rejoined. 'But you're standing over there . . . and this ain't exactly a pussy cat, you know.'

The powerful creature suddenly turned away from Dodo and moved toward the Doctor and Steven. In a feline way it rubbed against their legs.

'I hope you're satisfied now, my dear,' the Doctor said. 'Whatever it wants it seems to have a taste for all three of us!' Then he glared at the tiger and ejaculated: 'Shoo!'

It was an instinct that had made him use the word, but to his amazement and that of the others the tiger seemed to take notice of it.

It turned and, very sedately, moved away, finally

disappearing back under the cover of the trees.

All three sighed with relief, then stared at each other with incredulity.

'Cor ... that was a close one,' Dodo finally said.

'Yes!' Steven agreed. 'But I don't understand it, a tiger behaving like that. Maybe it was a tamed one.'

'Perhaps,' the Doctor observed. 'But hardly likely to that degree. It acted totally against the nature of the species.' He glanced around. 'I have that strange feeling about this place ... and the longer we are here, the stronger it becomes!'

Puzzled, they continued on their way.

In the Control Room Zentos moved towards the Commander, followed by a Monoid.

'There is something strange happening in the jungle,' he stated.

'What's that?' the Commander asked.

'There is a report from the Monoids. They have discovered the presence of intruders!'

'Intruders?' The Commander was puzzled and alarmed. 'But how can that be? How can they have entered?'

'I have no idea,' Zentos replied. 'I'll try and trace them.'

Mellium interjected: 'It's impossible for anything to be in the jungle that we don't know about. Where could they have come from?'

'I don't know,' Zentos answered. 'But according to the information they were somewhere in the co-ordinates ZH6 and OT274.'

Zentos moved to a scanner and operated the levers controlling it. Various images appeared on the screen, then located and held on a clearing in the jungle just as the Doctor, Dodo and Steven entered it. Zentos stood back and indicated the images to the Commander.

'There they are!' he exclaimed. 'Intruders!'

The Commander reacted in bewildered amazement.

'They look like human beings ... but it can't be!' he

18

exclaimed. 'We accounted for everyone ... and everything ... that should be in that area.'

Mellium's attention was caught by another screen which, locked into the primary one, had been searching the surrounding area in the jungle.

'Father, look! That could be their spaceship. But it's such an unusual design!'

The secondary screen was holding on the stationary TARDIS.

'Whoever ... whatever ... these beings are,' Zentos said, 'they must be arrested and brought here for immediate questioning!'

The Commander nodded. 'You're right.' Then he reflected on the nature of the command. 'But, Zentos ... not arrested! *Invited*!'

Zentos nodded and then started to leave, indicating to the Monoids to follow him.

The Doctor and his companions had moved out of the jungle and its sticky heat into the cool atmosphere of a cave. They adjusted their eyes to the comparative gloom within, then Dodo indicated the walls of the cave.

'Doctor, look at these fab pictures!'

'Fab?' the Doctor exclaimed. 'My child, one day we will have to do something about that English of yours. Most ... elastic ... the way you use it.'

'Elastic?'

'Very!' The Doctor peered closely at the cave drawings. 'Ah, yes. Interesting. Now look at that. It looks like a zebra with two heads.'

Steven moved across to peer over his shoulder. 'Two heads!?'

'Correct!' the Doctor confirmed.

'Maybe just the imagination of the artist,' Steven shrugged.

'Perhaps. And perhaps not. And if not ... what then?

H'm?' The Doctor was challenged by the thought. 'Think about it; we've already established this place as zoological. So why shouldn't there be such a thing as an animal with two heads. H'm?'

'No reason at all, I suppose,' Steven replied without conviction. 'But the more we see of this place the less like Earth it becomes.'

Dodo had moved back out of the cave and was standing on an escarpment from which she had a panoramic view of the jungle. Then her attention was caught by signs of movement near the TARDIS. Creatures were approaching it and cautiously surrounding it. She concentrated her gaze and reacted in horror when she began to make out what form of creatures they were. She yelped with terror and retreated back into the cave.

The Doctor stared at her in puzzlement.

'What is it, my child?' he asked, as she breathed hard, attempting to speak. 'You look as though you've seen a ghost!'

'No ...' Dodo managed to say, wiping at her nose with her hand, her handkerchief forgotten. 'If only they were just ghosts!'

'They?'

'Because, Doctor, if this *is* Earth, then it's no longer inhabited by human life!'

The Doctor and Steven stared at her in amazement. Then they went out to the escarpment and looked down on the jungle. Seeing what Dodo had seen, they pulled back.

'You're right, child,' the Doctor said. 'Terrifying! And those creatures ... whatever they are ... seem to be looking for us.'

'What do we do?' Steven asked.

'We must try and get back to the TARDIS and away from this place!' The Doctor led them cautiously out of the cave.

They started back into the jungle, using the cover of the trees and bushes, the Doctor moving ahead and then signalling to the others to follow him. But now they could hear the creatures around them, shuffling nearer, steadily closing in.

Suddenly Dodo stopped as her nose started itching. Her shoulders heaved as she attempted to contain herself, but her breathing came in shorter and shallower gasps.

'Quiet!' Steven hissed desperately.

'Trying to ...' she mumbled '... but my nose is running ...'

She pinched it and managed to contain the sneeze and they scrambled on. Reaching a high mound, the Doctor looked out at the terrain ahead of them. Then he paused, his face lighting up in triumph. He turned to the others as they joined him.

'Of course!' he said. 'I know where we are now. This – all this – is some kind of spaceship!'

'A spaceship?' Steven echoed.

They followed his gaze and in the distance saw a cluster of domed buildings. They stared at it in wonder and for one brief moment forgot their haste and their anxiety to escape.

But then Dodo brought her attention back to their immediate surroundings. She tugged at the Doctor's sleeve.

'Hey, Doctor,' she asked querulously. 'If this is a spaceship ... then what are they?'

From behind the concealing undergrowth the Monoids had risen to their feet, standing in a mute circle surrounding the Doctor and his two companions, who in turn stood transfixed, staring back at the scaly, reptilian creatures.

2

Capture

Much to their surprise, and despite the appearance of the Monoids, the Doctor and his companions had not been attacked by them.

Instead, the Monoids had merely signalled to them to follow them. In convoy they had started off through the jungle, passing the parked TARDIS, and had been led in the direction of the city of domed buildings.

Within, they had found it to be spacious and apparently well-organised. Vast spokes of corridors radiated out from the centre of the city, towards which they were led.

The Doctor was intrigued by the Monoids. He had attempted to communicate with them, but they had made no response to his overtures. Instead, by sign language, they urged their captives to keep walking.

Finally they reached a main door. A Monoid motioned toward it with a sweeping move of his arm and it slid open.

The Control Room.

The Doctor, Steven and Dodo relaxed immediately when they saw the humans inside. And they, for their part, studied the three of them intently as they entered.

'Crikey,' Dodo yelped. 'Civilisation!'

The Doctor cast her a sidelong glance.

'Perhaps,' he muttered. 'But the question still remains: what kind of civilisation?'

But if the Doctor was curious about their captors, it soon became evident that he and his companions would have some questions to answer. The Commander addressed them.

'We don't know how or exactly when you came here – but did you travel in that peculiar blue box device?'

'Yes,' the Doctor replied. 'That blue box, as you call it, is a spaceship.' Indicating his surroundings, he continued:

22

'Perhaps not on the scale of this one, but it travels just the same.'

'But why did you choose to come here?'

'We didn't,' Steven answered. 'Our spaceship chooses its own destination. Where it wants to go ... and in what period of time.'

The Commander laughed. 'You claim that that thing travels through both space and time?'

Dodo was peeved. 'It isn't a *thing*! It's the TARDIS! And it does have a mind of its own!'

The Commander and the other humans were still amused by this claim. 'I don't understand,' he said. 'Experiments to pass through the fourth dimension were undertaken in the twenty-seventh segment of time. They failed completely! So how could anything so – so crude and elementary succeed?'

'I don't know how the flipping thing works,' Dodo replied. 'The Doctor is the one who will tell you all about that.'

'Flipping?' The Commander looked queryingly at Zentos. 'I've never heard that word before.'

'Perhaps a code word,' Zentos suggested, frowning. 'We should be wary of these intruders.'

He stared searchingly at all three of them. Steven and Dodo stood before them, but the Doctor had wandered off, gazing curiously about him at the details of the Control Room.

The Doctor was fascinated by the banked display of instruments and observation screens, and by the way in which the humans and the Monoids worked together in such harmony.

'Extraordinary!' he exclaimed.

Mellium glanced up from her duties.

'What is?' she asked.

'Why, all this, my dear – and on such a scale. This spaceship is the largest I have known.'

'It is two thousand leagues long,' she replied proudly.

'Leagues?'

'Yes. Oh – the old measurements used to be in miles or kilometres. One league equals three of them; I forget which.'

'A mere trifle,' the Doctor shrugged. 'Whichever interpretation is used it still means that this is a giant spaceship.' He studied her appraisingly. 'What is your name, my dear?' he asked.

'I am Mellium, daughter of the First Commander.'

'First Commander?'

'He's over there, talking to your friends.'

'Oh, yes – that gentleman! Funny how times might change, but gentlemen always emerge.'

'That sounds like a class distinction of some kind. Something that was common in the old days.'

'But now no longer is?'

'No. Although we have certain titles aboard this ship they only indicate skills in certain duties.'

The Doctor indicated the Monoids: 'And those?'

'The Monoids? ... They have an equal ranking.'

'Among themselves, I presume,' the Doctor observed. 'But how, in the system of ranking, do they compare with your father ... and with you ... and the rest of your kind?'

'We try to treat them as equals, but they remain at some position between human kind and the animals that you have seen in the jungle.'

'I see. Equal ... but different!'

'Well, they are,' Mellium stated. 'For instance they have no language. They cannot speak because they have no vocal chords.'

'Ah, that explains it!'

'What?'

'When they escorted us from the jungle to this city I attempted to talk to them, but there was no response. I and my companions took it personally. We thought they didn't like us!'

'Oh, that would be nonsense!' Mellium responded. 'They are gentle creatures. They never give any trouble, and they are very happy working with us.'

'Glad to hear it!' the Doctor observed.

For a moment Mellium seemed uncertain, as though she had dismissed the Monoids too indifferently. 'They have made progress,' she went on. 'They have learned to understand us by reading our lips and a form of sign language. They can comprehend most of our written data, and several of them can even write it!'

'Ah, that is good to know. Soon you might have – what does one call them? – pen clubs!' Mellium shook her head, not quite understanding the phrase. 'But don't worry about it, my dear! Just treat it as the ramblings of an old wanderer!'

The Doctor smiled and moved away.

Steven spoke up: 'May I ask a question?'

'No!' Zentos snapped.

The Commander placed his hand reassuringly on Zentos's shoulder. 'Why not? We're all friends here.'

'Is this really a spaceship? This city and everything that we saw outside? The jungle, the cave, the animals, the flora – everything?'

'Yes, indeed,' the Commander answered. He indicated the bank of panels. 'Everything that you see on those screens is contained within our ship. The jungle, as you say, but also lakes and rivers, deserts ... and even simulated polar regions which are constantly bathed in snow and ice.'

Steven was amazed. 'But this must be the biggest ever ...' he faced them '... Look, who are you?'

'Like you, we are human beings. We come from the Earth.' Dodo indicated the Monoids.

'But what about them – where did they come from?'

'Ah, the Monoids!' The Commander smiled at them in a friendly manner. 'They came to the Earth many years ago, apparently from their own planet, which was dying. An obscure place. But they offered us their assistance and services in return for places on this spaceship.'

'Where are you going?' Steven asked.

'The planet Refusis,' replied the Commander. 'The Earth is also dying and now we have left it for the last time.'

'The last time?' asked Dodo in alarm.

'Yes. In a short time it will burn and be swallowed up in the gravity pull of the Sun.'

Steven tried to take this in, working out what the statement meant.

'Then we must have journeyed forward ... millions of years!'

Zentos interposed, 'You *are* human, I take it?'

'Of course!' Dodo replied hotly. 'Do you doubt it?'

Zentos ignored her and addressed the Commander. 'They could be Refusians, sent here to intercept us – to spy on us!'

'Refusians? Us!' Dodo retorted. 'We wouldn't know one end of ... of this Refusis from our elbow!'

'To try and sabotage our mission,' Zentos continued, 'they could have assumed human form. After all, we only know of the Refusians as intelligences that inhabit their planet. They may have the means to pass as human beings and attack us before we reach them!'

The Doctor had completed his very satisfying tour of the Control Room, taking in the advanced technical detail of its lay-out and smooth running operation. But now he returned to join his companions and the humans.

'Oh, rubbish! Rubbish! With all my imperfections, sir, I can assure you that if you were to cut my skin I would bleed. So would my two friends.'

'Right!' Steven assented.

Dodo's nose puckered again and before she could contain herself a sneeze burst forth. *'Atishoo!'*

'There, you see,' the Doctor stated. 'Complete with chills.'

'Chills?' Zentos was puzzled.

'Yes! A cold. Quite common to human beings.'

'Ah, yes, I have heard of them,' the Commander said. 'But cured and eradicated so long ago that we have completely forgotten what they were like. Fascinating! It's like history coming to life.' He took the Doctor's arm. 'Tell me, Doctor – if you cannot direct your space craft your journeys must have taken you to some strange places! Is that not so?'

'Correct!' affirmed the Doctor. 'And I could tell you some strange stories ...'

Zentos gave Steven a slow, appraising stare, then moved away to join Mellium at a scanner. She noticed his attitude and watched as he paused to speak to a Monoid in sign language. The Monoid nodded, then left the Control Room.

'What were you telling him?' Mellium asked.

'I wish to know more of the intruders' space craft. I know very little of them.'

'You don't trust them?'

'Your father seems to accept them, I agree,' Zentos replied. 'But I know that he has a simple faith, whereas I am suspicious. My faith is in my own eyes and ears ... and machines tell fewer lies than men.'

The Doctor had caught this last statement. 'Including the Daleks,' he ventured.

The Commander furrowed his brow. 'Ah – yes! Nero, the Trojan Wars, the Daleks! But all that happened in the First Segment of Time ... at the dawn of Man's history!'

The Doctor was curious. 'To use your own phrase, sir, what Segement are we in now?'

'The Fifty-Seventh!'

'Good gracious!' The Doctor made a hasty calculation on his finger tips. 'We must have jumped ... er ... ten million years! Incredible!'

'When do you expect to end your journey?' Steven asked.

'Not for a long time,' the Commander replied. 'Neither I nor my daughter Mellium, nor any of the beings here today, will ever see the planet. That pleasure is reserved for our children's children, many years hence.'

'How many?'

'Using your measurement of time – seven hundred years!'

The Doctor, Steven and Dodo caught their breath.

'Seven hundred . . . !' repeated the Doctor. 'But why travel so far?'

'Simple! Only Refusis has the same conditions that we had on Earth. Atmosphere, water, the right temperate zones.'

'Has anyone ever been there?' Steven asked.

'No! Our knowledge is based on audio space research.'

'H'm!' Steven ruminated. 'I suppose you had to bring at least two of everything?'

'Like the Ark?' Dodo asked.

'The Ark?'

'Yeah! You know, Noah's Ark. Everything in, two by two. A . . . a boat!'

The Commander shook his head. 'I'm afraid I don't know about that. But we do have the whole of the Earth's population aboard . . . human, animal and Monoid.'

'But where, sir?' the Doctor asked. 'I can see but a few . . .'

The Commander smiled.

'That is simply explained,' he said. 'We are the Guardians!' He motioned toward a special row of scanners. 'The rest are reduced in size to micro-cell dimensions and stored in those frames you see there . . .' They studied the screens and saw long caverns of floor to ceiling racks. '. . . and will be restored to normal size and life when our descendants make their landing on the new planet. In the meantime it is our duty to look after this spaceship and everyone and everything that travels in it, and to pass that task on through succeeding generations.'

'Quite a task!' the Doctor murmured in admiration.

'Each frame that you see on those screens contains a million people . . . other frames, more animals . . . and the Monoids have a special sector of their own.'

Dodo glanced at the reptilian creatures and sniffed. 'Accusing us of being Refusians or something strange . . . but I can't say that I care for the likes of them.'

'Judge not by appearances,' the Commander rejoined. 'The Monoids are a docile form of life and they obey our every whim without question.'

'I suppose I'll take your word for it,' Dodo replied. 'But I still wouldn't like to meet them alone on a dark night. I'd have an attack of the willies.'

'What strange expressions you use!'

'Something I've been trying to impress on the child, Commander,' the Doctor agreed. 'But I must say that I am very impressed by the way you have organised this ship.'

'Once the decision was taken for us to leave Earth it took five hundred ... er ... years to design and complete, with many feeder ships supplying this main one with everything that you see and that I have told you about.'

He turned to address his daughter: 'Mellium, why don't you take the young people through to the Great Hall and show them that, while the Doctor and I have a further chat?'

'Yes, Father, I'd love to,' Mellium agreed readily. She addressed Steven and Dodo. 'Please follow me.'

'Rightio!' Dodo assented and Steven nodded.

The three filed out of the Control Room while the Commander turned to the Doctor.

'And as for you, my dear friend,' he said, 'I am sure you would be much more interested in the technicalities of our ... what did they call it? ... our Ark!'

The Doctor nodded agreeably.

In the Energy Chamber the Doctor stood on an observation platform while the Commander indicated the mass of machinery with some pride.

'All energy aboard our spaceship – its propulsion force, its lighting, ventilation – comes from this chamber.'

'Magnificent!' the Doctor acceded. 'A bit different from the gadgetry I have to cope with on the TARDIS!'

'And this is only the main unit. There are two other similar chambers. Just in case of any malfunction, you understand.'

'Of course!' The Doctor pointed. 'I take it that those are the fuel tanks.'

'Yes. With enough reserves in them to cover five thousand

years of travel.'

'In the event that you don't find what you expect on the planet which is your present destination? Very wise. One can always travel in hope, but cautious planning is most advisable.'

The Commander studied him shrewdly.

'In that craft of yours have you ever travelled to the planet Refusis?'

'No.' The Doctor thought for a moment. 'But once, on a journey when I and my companions of that time landed on Shaba, we passed close by it.'

'Really? What impressions were you able to gain of it?'

'It seemed ... hospitable ... friendly ... even welcoming. I remember that at the time I wished we could have landed there instead of going on to Shaba.' He shrugged his shoulders. 'That was not a friendly place! Even before we landed they attacked us with some kind of rocket devices. Nasty things that locked into the heat emission of the TARDIS!' He grinned. 'But we managed to outwit them, ducking and weaving, then managing to turn one rocket against another.'

'In what I have learned of history I have never been able to understand the aggression of one species against another,' the Commander observed. 'Even to the point where it was exercised within species themselves and elements attacked their own kind.'

'But, Commander, you are a human being – and humans have always had aggression deeply embedded in their make-up.'

'Oh, no – no longer! Not since the Twentieth Segment of Time has there been any evidence of it or need for it.'

'But if that's the case, docility ... friendship ... call it what you want ... must have been bred into them?'

'It was! A full programme of genetic engineering achieved that result over a period of approximately one thousand years.'

'Amazing!'

'Of course, we have to maintain it ... and we do that by further control through our food sources.'

The Doctor was thoughtful. 'I'm told the Monoids are friendly ...'

'Yes. I have little knowledge of their past history, but they certainly behave now as we do.'

'... But what about the animal life in the jungle? The predators and their kind?'

'Ah, now that proved a little more difficult. The programme was extended to them and some re-education was achieved ...'

'Then that would explain the behaviour of the tiger!'

'... but a latent instinct of aggression has remained in them.' The Commander sighed. 'However, by the time we get to Refusis I am hoping that we ... our descendants ... will have achieved total success among them, as well.' Then he gestured to the Doctor to follow. 'Come – I will show you our water purifying system. I'm sure you will find that interesting, too.'

The two men moved away.

Zentos walked over to join Manyak, who was on duty at his section of screen monitors.

'Where is the Commander now?' he asked.

'He was in the Energy Chamber with the one they call the Doctor. Now they are on their way to the Purification Plant.'

'The Commander is a wise man,' Zentos observed. 'But I think too trusting.' He glanced at the screens. 'I think I was right to demand that the intruders' spaceship be investigated. Are the Monoids anywhere near it?'

Manyak flipped a lever and made an adjustment on one of the screens. 'Yes! They're approaching the glade where it rests.'

On the screen a party of Monoids could be seen making their way through the jungle toward the parked TARDIS.

'Good!' said Zentos with satisfaction. 'Then soon we might

have some answers about the true origins of the intruders, and any plans that they might have!' Then he glanced at other screens. 'We know where the Commander is, but what about Mellium and the others?'

'Here!' Manyak answered. 'They are just about to enter the Great Hall.'

Steven and Dodo marvelled at the immense size of the Great Hall the moment they entered it. Its convex roof was at least a hundred and fifty metres above the floor and galleries ran along its walls as far as the eye could see. Guardians and Monoids could be seen strolling along the galleries, obviously relaxing in their moments off duty.

Fountains were positioned here and there in the Hall, along with rockeries that supported colourful plants and flowers. There was an air of tranquillity here, sharply contrasting with the atmosphere of the jungle and even the Control Room.

Save at its centre. Here a party of Guardians and Monoids were at work, concentrating on the task of creating a statue. So far only the feet of the statue were complete and the mixed team of workers were erecting scaffolding that would take them higher.

'What's that?' enquired Steven.

'Our statue,' Mellium replied proudly. 'Homo Sapiens. Started on Earth and due to be completed, according to our planning edicts, just before the landing on Refusis.'

'Seven hundred years to build one blooming statue.' Dodo was amazed and moved closer to look at it. 'Coo . . . we could have knocked one of these up in half the time.'

'The time-span is purposely worked out so that down through the years there will be an occupation available other than the routine tasks.'

'I can understand that,' Steven conceded. Then he glanced away to see Dodo climbing the scaffolding to reach a brick. 'Dodo!'

'What's it made of?' Dodo asked. 'You can't scratch this . . .

it's too hard!'

'It's a substance called Gregarian Rock, especially imported from the planet of that name. It is very hard and will resist any conditions into which it is taken.'

'You mean ... like diamonds?' Dodo scrambled back down.

'Diamonds? Oh, the Earth exhausted its diamond reserves a long time ago,' Mellium replied. 'But from what I remember of their recorded chemical make-up, this stone is much harder than that.'

'Harder?' Dodo was impressed. 'In that case it must be very valuable, so if you've got any chippings to spare we could load some into the old TARDIS!'

In the glade where the TARDIS stood the party of Monoids approached and surrounded it.

The leader among them reached for the door to open it ... but then suddenly its hand went to its face as it reacted to the sudden violent onslaught of a virus.

It gasped, the first sound it had ever made, then tried to hang onto the door in order to stay upright. But the virus was fast-acting and the creature staggered and fell to the ground.

The other Monoids clustered round, puzzled. They attempted to haul the fallen one to its feet, but when this failed they picked it up and carried it away out of the glade.

The Commander was showing the Doctor a flight leveller in the Control Room when Zentos approached.

'Commander, excuse me for a moment. A strange disease ... a fever ... is spreading among the Monoids!'

'What? What kind of disease?'

'Commander, your voice – it sounds strange.'

Zentos glanced at the Doctor, who nodded. 'I noticed it a few moments ago,' he said. 'The Commander was kindly showing me everything when his voice suddenly became husky.' He turned to the Commander. 'Commander, listen to me ...'

'What ...?' What's that ...? I ... I can hardly hear what you are saying.' The Commander pulled at his clothes, attempting to loosen them. 'It ... it's so hot ...'

He was gasping and the Doctor reached forward to hold him and save him from falling. But Zentos pushed him aside and grasped the Commander instead, easing him to the floor. As he did so, Mellium re-entered the Control Room, followed by Steven and Dodo.

'What's happened?' Mellium asked in alarm.

'He has a strange fever ... a fever brought by the strangers.' As Mellium approached her father he held her back. 'Stay away from him, Mellium.'

Dodo knelt down quickly and placed her hand on the Commander's forehead. 'It's nothing to worry about,' she announced firmly. 'His temperature is a bit high, that's all. It's only a cold.'

The door of the Control Room opened and a conveyor was driven in by a Monoid, with the stricken Monoid, who had collapsed near the TARDIS, lying on it.

The Doctor glanced round and his face took on a worried expression. Then he addressed Steven. 'Do you realise what this means, my dear boy?'

'It's nothing to worry about,' Steven assured him. 'Like Dodo said; it's only a cold, that's all.'

'All! ... These people – this generation – have never experienced the common cold. For the simple reason that it was wiped out many generations ago before they were born. They have no resistance to it!'

'What?' In turn, Steven grew alarmed. 'Then what can we do?'

'I don't know! All I know is that it could be fatal to them. And, if so ... we might be blamed!' Impatiently the Doctor banged his hands together. 'Yes, it's all our fault and I should have foreseen it!'

Zentos pointed at the Doctor and addressed the others.

'Did you hear that? I tried to warn all of you and the Commander! I told you these beings were evil!'

'But it wasn't my fault!' Dodo protested. 'How was I supposed to know?'

Manyak had walked over to the conveyor to study the sick Monoid. Then he looked up, shaking his head. 'This Monoid ... he's dead!'

There was a murmur of agitation as others, including Monoids, gathered round to confirm his finding. Then quickly backed away when they found it to be true.

Zentos pointed to the Doctor, Steven and Dodo and called out in a commanding voice: 'Seize them!' The others needed no second bidding; they rushed up and grasped the three firmly. 'Listen, all of you! The mission we are engaged upon ... the mission we and our children and our children's children have to carry out ... is in danger! Put in jeopardy by these intruders in our midst! By special Galactic Law they must be taken into custody!'

'What's that!' the Doctor demanded.

'And later they will be made to suffer for the crime that they have committed!' When the Doctor and the others attempted to protest he brushed their words aside. 'Take them away!'

The Doctor, Steven and Dodo were hastily bundled out of the Control Room, still proclaiming their innocence, but only too aware now that they were surrounded by hostile beings, both human and Monoid.

Mellium, uncertain of her feelings, turned to Zentos. 'But what about my father?' she asked.

Zentos stared at the shivering Commander and then shook his head. 'He may well die! ... But, then, so might all of us.' He pulled a lever on a main scanner and studied the image that appeared on it. 'In which case it was pointless leaving!'

On the scanner the Earth could be seen. An Earth already marked with scorches where the solar flares of the Sun had started to lick it, burning off forests, and sending dense clouds of smoke into the atmosphere.

3

The Plague

'What do you think they'll do to us, Doctor?' Steven asked.

'I'm not sure, my dear boy,' the Doctor replied. 'We'll just have to wait and see.'

He studied the place in which he, Steven and Dodo had been incarcerated.

A medium-sized room with plain walls and simple benches. Sprucely clean, as was everything else on the Ark... but this was their jail.

Dodo sniffed, feeling sorry for herself. 'If I had known it was going to be like this I wouldn't have come.' She wiped her nose. 'And as for them catching cold... well, it's all my fault.'

'Well, you did come, child, so it's too late to worry about that! Stop snivelling!'

'I'm not snivelling. It's me nose running again.' Then she took a deep breath. 'Anyway, I'm starting to feel a little better now ... not that I suppose anyone cares!'

'But of course they care! They may be cautious ... uncertain ... frightened ... but if there is one thing I've learnt about them already, they care!'

'What makes you so sure?'

'Because they care about everything that happens on this spaceship. After all the trouble they've gone to, planning it and building it and gambling all their hopes of survival on it, they care about everything that happens to it.' He glanced at Steven, who was prowling about the room, running his fingers over the walls and around the door jambs. 'No use trying to escape from this place, I'm afraid. The way they've constructed it there would be no margin for physical escape of that kind.'

'I suppose you're right,' Steven agreed. Resignedly he sat down on one of the benches. 'But when you mention *physical* escape ... might there not be another way out for us, Doctor?'

'None that I can think of at this moment. I'm sure the Commander and that chap Zentos and the rest of them have ensured all avenues of metaphysical security.'

Dodo looked at Steven. 'Were you thinking that the Doctor might get us out of here like ... in a puff of smoke?'

'I've heard of people who specialised in escaping from some very tight spots. They were so good they made a living at it.'

'Ah, music hall artistes for the most part,' the Doctor reminded him. 'But that was illusion disguised as reality. Whereas reality for one of them ... a chap named Houdini ... met him once, on my travels ... quite a nice fellow ... reality for him was death, when one of his tricks went wrong. He was chained, immersed upside down in water, and was supposed to free himself and get out. But, unfortunately, he failed ... and was drowned!'

Dodo shivered. 'Then let's don't try anything like that.' She sighed. 'But that lot out there – the people and the Monoids – will they blame me if my cold spreads?'

'Now you must not worry, my dear,' the Doctor tried to reassure her. 'It's not your fault at all. If it's anybody's, it's mine!'

'But do you think this has happened before?' Steven asked. 'That an infection was carried from one age to another ... or even one planet to another?'

'Don't waste your time with conjecture!' the Doctor retorted. 'Though I must say the thought of it and what it might eventually mean is too horrifying! ... Scientists in the past have tried to work out the consequences of such an eventuality. But we are *experiencing* it, here and now.'

'Maybe it'll just go away,' Dodo ventured.

'That depends: number one, on the strength of the virus; number two, on whether they have any latent immunity despite the ... er ... Segments of Time since their forebears last suffered it.'

'If it's half as bad as my cold was it will knock 'em for six,'

Dodo sniffed.

'Oh, for heaven's sake, do use your handkerchief, child,' the Doctor snapped, irritably. 'H'm! If you had used it more often when we were in the jungle then perhaps this wouldn't have happened.'

Dodo pulled a face. 'I knew you'd blame me, no matter what you said originally.' She sniffed again and this time wiped her nose with her handkerchief. 'And anyway, it's not me nose that's running any more. I'm crying this time.'

The Doctor relaxed, altering his tone. 'Then you had better rest, Dorothea . . .'

'Dodo!'

'. . . whatever. Rest and regain your strength because you're far from cured!' He turned away from her and paced restlessly. 'Oh, if only those wretched Guardians would let us out of here, we might be able to help them, h'm?'

He stared in frustration at the walls that imprisoned them.

A procession wound its way through the Great Hall.

At its centre was the conveyor on which rested the body of the dead Monoid, encased in a simple shroud.

The accompanying Guardians and Monoids moved along without open expressions of emotion of any kind. Bystanders lined their route and on the galleries above them more spectators were gathered. Nowhere was there an open display of grief, for this would have been alien to them. But a quietly contained concern could be felt.

The conveyor and its cargo glided out of the Great Hall into the Launching Area.

Here were bays that contained space launchers of varying sizes. Among them, a single occupancy size.

The body of the Monoid was lifted into it and the launcher eased into an expulsion cavity.

A Guardian made sure that loading was correct, then reached for the firing button. He hesitated. Instead, he offered the task to a Monoid who had accompanied him.

The Monoid indicated his thanks for the honour by an inclination of his head. Then he stepped forward and pressed the button.

There was a loud hiss. They all looked up at a nearby screen monitor and saw the launcher and its dead cargo being ejected, speeding away from the Ark and disappearing into the void of space.

The task done, they turned and made their way back to the Great Hall.

In the Great Hall a Guardian suddenly choked and collapsed, falling to the floor. A Monoid went over to assist him ... but in turn was suddenly convulsed by an attack and fell alongside the Guardian.

The others watched, bewildered, uncertain what to do. The event itself, and the reaction to it, were caught by a Seeing Eye.

In the Control Room, Zentos and Manyak had seen the events in the Great Hall relayed onto a monitor screen.

'Two more who have fallen victims of the plague!' Zentos observed, a note of anger edging into his voice. 'The spread of the virus is not showing any signs of abating.' Worriedly, he asked, 'How many victims does that make so far?'

'Twenty-three!' Manyak informed him.

'And all within a few hours!' He glanced at another monitor screen. 'Look!'

The screen relayed the scene near the parked TARDIS. Another Monoid could be seen, suddenly gasping and vainly struggling to breathe. Then it, like the others in the Great Hall, staggered and collapsed.

'Another victim! Twenty-four!' He studied the picture intently. 'He isn't moving. It looks as though that's another Monoid death. Thank heavens no Guardians have died so far.'

39

'What will happen if any do?' Manyak asked.

'It would be disaster!' Zentos replied. 'Each individual has his allotted task! No-one has foreseen anything like this eventuality.'

'There must be something that we can do.'

'Our microbiologists are trying to find the answer. One of them, Rhos, is with the Commander now in a special isolation unit that he has organised.'

The isolation unit was like the jail in which the Doctor and his companions were imprisoned. It was bare of furnishings, its walls scrubbed and polished clean.

Rhos, the microbiologist, was attending to the Commander, who was lying back on a plain slab. Mellium was hovering at his side and a Monoid was mopping his brow. All three wore protective helmets.

The Commander was moaning and breathing in quick, shallow gasps. He was sweating and shivering, the whole of his body quivering under the onslaught of the virus.

Rhos checked the Commander's temperature, then motioned to Mellium to follow him as he retreated to the far side of the isolation unit.

'Is there nothing you can do?' Mellium asked anxiously.

Rhos shook his head: 'Unfortunately the art of conquering this type of fever was lost long ago. As far as I can recall from my readings, that happened in the Primal Wars of the Tenth Segment.'

The Commander stirred and made an attempt to pull himself together and control the shaking in his limbs.

'Mellium . . .' he whispered.

She turned to face him. 'Yes, Father?'

'. . . I seem to be drifting from moments of unconsciousness to moments of sudden clarity. It . . . it is a very strange . . . and exhausting . . . experience.'

'Father, perhaps you shouldn't talk!'

'I must . . . I must try.' He took a deep, steadying breath.

'Promise me that ... that no matter what happens to me ...'

'What?'

'Anything ... to me ... or any of the others ... that you will make sure that the voyage continues ...'

'Of course,' Mellium replied. 'But something will happen that will make everything all right for you ... for all of us!'

'What happens to me is not important. It is the voyage ... the mission ... that counts. That's all!' He paused, struggling for breath, then continued. 'Its completion ... the end of the long journey that we have started ... and the landing of our descendants on the planet Refusis. That is the only thing that is important!'

Mellium nodded. 'Yes, father. We know!'

The Commander eased back on the slab, his eyes closing. Rhos hurried over to examine him, Mellium at his elbow.

'He is resting,' Rhos said. 'Probably the best thing for him, giving us time ... time to think ... and try to remember.'

Mellium nodded, then turned to watch the Monoid who was, so gently, helping to nurse her father. She smiled her thanks to him, but he hardly noticed as he continued attending to the Commander.

In the Control Room, Zentos addressed the Guardians and Monoids, commanding their attention: 'Listen to me, all of you!'

They crowded around him and he continued. 'Guardians ... Monoids! Before it is too late we must make the intruders answer for the terrible crime that they have committed!'

There was a general chorus of assent.

Zentos continued: 'A hearing will commence at once! As Deputy Commander I will put the charges ... but in keeping with Galactic Law, will anyone speak for the prisoners?'

They glanced at one another uncertainly. Then Manyak stepped forward. 'Yes. I will!'

Mellium, re-entering the Control Room, immediately added her support.

'And so will I! My father would wish that. His only desire would be that justice should be done and a sensible solution to this crisis be found!'

From the moment Zentos stepped forward with his proclamation, all events within the Control Room were relayed through the communications system to all points of the Ark – echoing in the Great Hall, at various listening posts in the jungle, in the isolation unit where the Commander nodded his head in agreement with his daughter's statement, and in the jail where the Doctor, Dodo and Steven were confined.

They looked up, startled, on hearing the relayed voices, then listened intently to Zentos's opening statement.

'In order that Earth life shall be extended and perpetuated through the success of this spaceship's mission, the Guardians shall have total powers to punish or restrain any life forms that threaten its possible success, by expulsion from this ship, miniaturisation, or such lesser penalty as shall be deemed fit!'

The Doctor grasped his lapels thoughtfully on hearing these opening remarks. 'Ah! So that's it! Some sort of trial!'

'And we are the accused,' Steven realised.

'I knew no good was going to happen today,' Dodo moaned. 'As I recall it's Friday the thirteenth!'

'Maybe it was,' the Doctor retorted. 'But we are in a different Segment, so perhaps that doesn't apply.'

Then he looked up as he realised that he was being directly addressed by Mellium via the communications system.

'Doctor, Manyak and I believe your story. We've offered to speak in your defence, but at least one of you must give evidence.'

'Why, yes – of course!' the Doctor answered, realising that the relay system was two-way.

Steven stumbled to his feet. 'I must go!'

'What?'

'I must do something . . . anything to get out of this room. It . . . it's stifling in here.' Steven moved toward the door. 'And I might be able to show them how stupid they are, wasting their time making charges and speeches like the one that Guardian just made.'

'But, my dear boy, advocacy is a special art . . .'

'Telling the truth isn't! And if I can persuade them, I might help get you started on finding a cure.'

'Very well, then,' the Doctor agreed. 'If only they will listen.'

'They will probably want you to speak afterwards, Doctor,' Dodo ventured.

'My dear, I only want to help.' He addressed the relay system. 'Guardians, one of our number – young Steven – is prepared to enter your court. All he asks is a fair and open-minded hearing.'

The reply came back immediately.

'Very well, then,' Zentos said. 'Let him come forward.'

The door of the jail-room slid open and Steven moved through it and into . . .

. . . the Control Room, where he was immediately ushered into a cage that was obviously designed to serve as a dock for the accused.

Steven gazed round at the assembled Guardians and Monoids in the Control Room. They seemed to crowd around him and press in on him, hostile and accusing. He wasn't sure whether it was fear or something else . . . but sweat gathered on his brow and the words that were addressed to him sounded hollow and echoing.

It was Zentos who spoke. 'My contention is that it was no accident that you came here, as you and your companions previously stated. It is my belief that you came here intentionally to spread the disease.'

'Nonsense!' Steven retorted.

'And by so doing, cause this disaster!'

43

'But that ... that is utter nonsense.'

Zentos pointed at Steven challengingly.

'It is my belief that you are agents of the planet toward which we are proceeding. And that you were sent by the Refusians to destroy us.'

'Why? We're human beings, like you. Why should we?'

'That is the crux of my argument,' replied Zentos. 'Do you expect us to believe that nonsense that you, in that ridiculous machine you call the TARDIS, managed to travel through time?' He addressed the court. 'Guardians, Monoids, these beings, whatever they are, place a heavy strain on our credulity!'

'That's not very difficult,' Steven retorted. 'If your medical records are anything to go by this Segment of time, instead of being one of the most advanced in knowledge, is one of the most backward.'

There was an immediate reaction, a murmuring of protest from the Guardians and the Monoids gathered in the Control Room.

In the jail-room the Doctor sighed. 'I warned him that advocacy was a special art – one that often calls for delicacy rather than the heavy hammer.'

'Oh, I don't know,' Dodo retorted stoutly. 'I think Steven is really giving them what for!'

'I suppose one could say that,' said the Doctor drily. He observed her shrewdly. 'But things might be worse.'

'How?'

'It could be *you* in there, defending us – and in that case ... h'm!' He left the thought unspoken. Dodo pouted in silent reply.

Zentos returned to the attack against Steven. 'We can cope with most things known in the Fifty-Seventh Segment of Time, but not with a strange disease, brought by you and your kind as agents of the intelligences that inhabit Refusis.'

'Are you still on about that?' Steven demanded. 'I've told you before – we know nothing of that planet.'

'My instinct, every fibre of my being, tells me different-ly ...'

'That, unfortunately, leads me to only one conclusion ...'

'What's that?'

'... that man, even in this day and age, hasn't altered his basic nature at all. You still fear the unknown, like everyone else before you.'

In the isolation unit the Commander had been able to follow the course of some of the trial, despite his occasional lapses into coma, and on hearing this he grabbed the arm of the microbiologist, Rhos.

'That's true!' he cried out.

Rhos and the attendant Monoid restrained him as he attempted to sit up. But his spirit fought back as he listened to the developing trial.

'That still won't stop me from combatting you,' said Zentos.

'How?' Steven asked. 'By destroying us? By ejecting us into space?'

'If that is the voted judgment of this hearing, yes!'

Manyak moved forward. 'Steven ...'

'Yes?'

'Prove to us your good faith! Would your friend, the one you call the Doctor, have any knowledge of how to deal with this fever?'

'Yes, he probably would if you'd let him out of that cell so that he could have a chance to experiment.'

'I have the feeling that you are correct.'

In the jail-room the Doctor observed: 'Well, at least one or two of them are on our side. So all is not lost.'

Zentos returned to the attack. 'I'm sure he'd love to try – so

that he can spread the fever further and faster.' He appealed
to the others. 'Guardians, are we to be fooled by such tricks?
Are we to be taken in by such nonsense?'

There was an immediate chorus of 'No' from all sides.

The Doctor heard this emphatic majority response and
sighed. 'Maybe I spoke too soon.'

'These creatures may have the appearance of human
beings,' Zentos continued. 'But I think they are something
entirely different ... and they should be punished.'

'That's right!' came a baying chorus, and one of the
Guardians stepped forward with the demand: 'Eject them!'

'But I ... I don't think you've *proved* any kind of a case,'
protested Steven, wiping his brow. 'It ... it's nothing but ...
but guessing ...' The Control Room was swimming around
before his eyes and the chattering, clamouring voices were
echoing in his head.

He grasped at the bars of the cage, attempting to stay
upright. But his words trailed away and the strength ebbed
from his body as he collapsed to the floor.

The Doctor had heard the tremulous, faltering voice.
Worried, he addressed Dodo. 'This trial is more serious than
I suspected ... and there is something wrong with Steven.'

'Do you think he may have caught the fever?'

'I think so, my dear. It appears that this infection is more
virulent than I suspected.'

In the Control Room there was further consternation among
the Guardians and the Monoids when they saw what had
happened to Steven. They were curious, and at the same time
alarmed. Manyak seized on this moment of uncertainty to
address them again.

'Guardians! Monoids! There is something ...'

A chorus of voices tried to drown him out, but Zentos held
up his hand.

'Let Manyak speak. After all, this is a fair trial.'

'Thank you, Zentos,' Manyak acknowledged as the noise of protest abated. 'My appeal for reason in this matter is simple and direct. The Doctor and his companions have not denied that they have brought the fever among us. They say it was an accident – and I believe them ...'

'So do I,' Mellium interjected.

'If they were agents of the Refusians they could have achieved interference and sabotage in a much simpler way, and without exposing themselves to this danger.'

'But perhaps that was their ploy,' Zentos suggested.

'I don't believe that. In any case, I have another point: the fever is here – it is a fact – and we cannot deal with it. They might be the only ones who can do something about it.'

'I wish I could believe that,' Zentos countered. 'But my instincts still say otherwise.'

'And if they are the only ones who can find a cure, what would be the value of expelling them from our spaceship?'

The Commander's voice was heard interjecting: 'None at all! If Manyak and my daughter can see that, why can't the rest of you?'

For a moment they seemed uncertain, caught between the opposing arguments. But as they murmured together, debating the points, another Guardian, a young man, entered the Control Room.

'Listen to me!' he called out. 'I've just had further bad news. One of our kind, a fellow Guardian, has died from the fever!'

Immediately the debating of the issue ceased.

'Do you want to hear more?' Zentos asked. 'Never mind the arguments of the defendant because they mean nothing, now that one of our own kind has died.' He faced them with a final challenge: 'So, Guardians, what is your answer to the charge? Do you find them guilty or not guilty?'

There was a mixed reaction to his question. Some cried 'Not guilty', but the majority drowned them out with their declamation of 'Guilty!'

'And by your vote do you agree that we exact the full penalty demanded by the special Galactic Law?' Again the mixed reaction, with those in favour of the motion drowning out those who thought otherwise. 'So be it! I formalise sentence in the following manner. The intruders will be taken from here and placed in an expulsion chamber ... and be cast out into space! And our friends, the Monoids, in consideration of the fact that one of their number was the first to die, will have the honour of executing the sentence!'

The Monoids bowed in grateful thanks.

Mellium went over to Manyak. 'The verdict is wrong!'

'I know,' he replied. 'But there is nothing that we can do about it.'

The Doctor clasped his hands together. 'Well, that's it, my dear Dodo. Not only the end of the Earth, but the end of us!'

'But, Doctor, something must be wrong with Steven. He's let them talk, and he hasn't said so much as a boo to their verdict.'

'You're right, my dear. Most unlike him after that splendid, cantering start!' He addressed the relay system. 'Now I demand to be heard!' he called out. 'How can you expect that young man out there to present a defence when he is so obviously ill himself? H'm!?'

Zentos replied over the relay system.

'The verdict has been pronounced ...'

'Oh, I thought you argued your case very well, young man. But does it count when it is against a *sick* man?' With satisfaction the Doctor heard uncertainty being echoed in the Control Room. 'The verdict has been returned, I agree, but I must beg leave to lodge an appeal!'

Again, the murmuring sounds of doubt.

'Well?'

For a moment there was silence, then the door of the jail-room slid open. The Doctor passed quickly through it, followed by Dodo.

*

In the Control Room Guardians and Monoids fell back as the Doctor and Dodo entered, as though afraid of getting too near them.

Except for Mellium and Manyak. They hastened to the Doctor's side, while Dodo quickly went over to Steven in the cage.

She placed her hand on his head. 'Yes, Doctor, he is running a high fever.'

'More of it,' Zentos cried. 'You and your party have been sentenced to expulsion into outer space!'

'I know, I know. I heard all that,' the Doctor rejoined. 'But if you do that you will be condemning yourselves and everything aboard this ship. Trust me! Help me! Help me to find a cure for this sickness that is beginning to decimate your numbers.'

'Perhaps there is no cure,' Zentos replied. 'Something that you have already seen to.'

'No!' The Doctor took up the challenge. 'Dodo, come here.' Puzzled, Dodo went to his side. 'You saw this child before, you heard her sniffles and her sneezing. You remember that her brow was fevered and hot. Well, feel it now!'

Zentos turned his gaze on her, but remained where he was, refusing to take the challenge and the risk. Instead, Mellium stepped forward and placed her hand on Dodo's forehead.

'It's true!' she exclaimed. 'Just as the Doctor says. Her brow is cool.'

'But that could be trickery ...'

'Nonsense!' the Doctor replied. 'It is explained by the fact that the child has antibodies in her system which have fought off the fever. And while that young man over there ...' he indicated Steven '... is suffering at this moment, his system will fight back and cure itself in time.'

'But what about us?' Zentos asked doubtfully.

'You're different, your generation no longer has the antibodies, and that is the nub of the matter. We must work to develop them and introduce them among you so that you will

49

be able to fight back of your own accord.'

'It makes sense to me,' Manyak said.

'It will mean hard work. It will need the efforts of everyone, both Guardians and Monoids, if we are to tackle the task.'

'Look at it another way,' Mellium implored Zentos. 'What have we got to lose by doing as he says?'

The Commander's husky voice could be heard on the relay system. 'Well spoken, my child.'

'I'm not so sure,' Zentos said. But then he looked round at the assembled Guardians and Monoids, sensing uncertainty among them. 'But if you – all of you – have changed your minds, then the sentence could be reversed. We might be able to take a chance on them . . . as long as we keep a careful eye on what they are doing.'

The murmuring of debate started up again. Then a senior Guardian quickly communicated with a group of Monoids and turned to face Zentos.

'We have decided to grant the appeal,' he stated. 'It may be our only way out. And the Monoids agree with us.'

Zentos bowed as he acceded to the change.

'Then, I so agree. I think we are taking a chance . . . but perhaps it is the only one we have.'

The voice of the Commander addressed them: 'I am glad you have reached that decision before I had to intervene and order it! Now the Doctor and his friends must be given every assistance, every facility, in order to help them with their research. And I am relying on you, Zentos, to support them with your organising skills while I . . . while I must continue to rest.' The voice picked up again for a moment. 'As for you, Doctor . . . good luck!'

The Doctor bowed respectfully, almost in the manner of the Monoids whenever they expressed their thanks.

4

The Fight Back

Steven had been moved from the Control Room back to the jail-room. Only now its door had been left open and it was being used as a sick bay.

The Doctor hovered over his patient, flanked by Dodo and Mellium. For a moment he pondered, then delivered his first instruction.

'Cover him with something to keep him warm,' he said.

'But why?' Mellium asked, confused. 'He is already hot and sweating.'

'I know it may not make sense to you, my dear, but extra warmth will help break the fever. See how he shivers. Although his temperature is high he is actually moving through hot and cold cycles. That is one of the contradictory symptoms of this illness.' He glanced round. 'Where is that other young lady?'

'Do you mean me, Doctor?' Dodo asked.

'Yes. Now, go to the TARDIS and bring these things back for me.' He had hastily written a list of items on a sheet of paper.

'The TARDIS? Me – alone?'

'Ask for help, for someone to go with you. That young man who spoke up in Steven's defence . . .' He turned to Mellium. 'What was his name?'

'Manyak,' Mellium replied.

'Yes, Manyak! Now get along with you! And hurry!'

'OK,' Dodo replied, setting out.

'*What* did you say?'

'OK!'

'That's what I thought.' He sighed. 'Why I should worry about something like that at a time like this, I don't know. But I do. And once we have resolved this dilemma we'll have to tackle the crisis of your communication.'

'Me what?!'

'Never mind. Get out of here. In other words ... skidaddle!'

Dodo shrugged and started out. As she did so, the microbiologist, Rhos, entered.

'My staff and I are ready to give all the help we can,' he said. He looked at Steven, who had been covered in sheets of thermo-foil by Mellium. 'You wish to make him *warmer*?'

'Yes! And everyone else aboard this spaceship who has been struck down by the virus. Guardians, Monoids – oh, and the Commander. Do that at once.'

'Yes, Doctor,' Mellium replied and immediately left the room. The Doctor turned to Rhos.

'Now this virus. Basically it's a germ that lurks in the nervous system ...' He glanced at Rhos enquiringly. 'I take it that you still do have a nervous system in your physical make-up?'

'Yes.'

'Just wondered. So much else has changed I thought perhaps ... but never mind. You have a nervous system. That means it can be attacked ... and has been. Our reply is to identify the type of germ and then develop the agent that will put up a defence against it.'

'The antibodies that you mentioned?'

'Yes,' replied the Doctor. 'Oh, this is going to be fun! Working together like the Curies or some such.'

'Curies? Is that a species, or a race of beings?'

The Doctor shook his head. 'Oh, no! Marie and Pierre Curie – a husband and wife team of scientists of the nineteenth century ...' His voice trailed away in the face of the blank, uncomprehending stare that Rhos gave him. 'Anyway, what we seek to develop now will be called a vaccine ...'

'Vaccine?'

'Yes. A natural compound derived from animal blood. We need only take single specimens and then we can release the animals again. And we also need plant derivitives. Then, mixed and prepared in the right order, they will give us the basis of the vaccine we require.'

'That means a large hunt and search will have to be mounted,' Rhos reflected.

'Yes. I told you the task won't be easy, and it may not even work the first time. But that chap Zentos should be able to organise something. In fact I think he'd be rather good at that kind of thing.'

'I'll speak to him right away.'

Rhos turned and left the room. The Doctor examined Steven and his expression of concern deepened as he discovered that the fever was still raging and that Steven's temperature had risen even higher.

Zentos had divided the jungle up into zones, to give maximum coverage, and deployed pairs of hunters, each pair comprising a Guardian and a Monoid.

A couple of them closed in on a goat. Hearing them coming it darted away to find cover, but the Guardian signalled to the Monoid to move in behind the copse where it was sheltering. The Guardian called out, beating on the foliage while he pursued the goat, driving it straight into the arms of the waiting Monoid.

He held it by its horns as it struggled, seeking to break free, then twisted it gently so that it was brought to the ground, its legs still kicking in futile protest. The Guardian joined the Monoid and together they prised open the goat's jaws. The Guardian examined the frothing tongue and then reached into the goat's throat with a swab-probe, extracting saliva. Satisfied, he placed the saliva in a container. In the same moment the Monoid released the goat, which staggered to its feet and then bounded gratefully away.

Other pairs of Guardians and Monoids were combing the jungle and hunting down various animals, birds and insects. In some cases they obtained just the saliva; in others, they carried out small operations to remove blood samples.

Plants were also harvested, bundled and carried back to the city. By the end of the day the Doctor was informed that the search was yielding the required results.

His reaction: 'More! More of the same thing and other varieties as well! We must have every possible combination of ingredients to arrive at our final compound.'

Patiently and efficiently, the Guardians and the Monoids carried out his bidding, searching high and low for at least one specimen of each life form that teemed in the jungle.

In the TARDIS Dodo and Manyak collected together the items the Doctor had demanded.

'A tray from the shelf near the Space Longitude Indicator,' Dodo read out. She indicated. 'I think that's this one here. Looks like the sort of thing dentists use in their surgeries.' She placed it on a pile with other items already collected.

'Dentists?' Manyak asked.

'You know – those horrible people who drill your teeth and insist on talking to you when your mouth is already numb from the stuff they inject so you're not supposed to feel a thing.' She shivered. 'Yuk!'

'But why would they want to drill your teeth?' asked Manyak in astonishment.

'To put in fillings . . . you know, take out bad parts and then put in good bits. Or so they say.' Manyak still shook his head, obviously baffled. Dodo was intrigued by this. 'Do you mean to say that you don't have dentists?' she asked. 'That your teeth never ache?'

Manyak shook his head. 'No!'

'Hey, yours isn't such a bad life, after all!' Then she again consulted her list. 'A thermometer – centigrade and fahrenheit readings – in a drawer near the Main Thrust Control.' She looked around. 'I think this is the Control . . .' she opened a drawer '. . . and here's the thermometer!'

Manyak watched her and gazed around in amazement at

the interior of the TARDIS, as he had done from the moment he had entered it.

'This ... this machine ... the thought of it travelling anywhere defeats me!' he marvelled. 'And according to all three of you, it not only travels through space but through time?'

'That's right!' Dodo replied cheerfully.

'Frankly, we didn't believe ... but there's one thing I cannot reason out, now that I am aboard.'

'What's that?'

'Well, from the outside it's the size of a box, only large enough to contain one, perhaps two, people. But once inside there seems to be room for six – maybe ten – or even more!'

'Ah!' Dodo exclaimed. 'Lots of people have been fooled by that. But the explanation is simple ...'

'It is?'

'Optical illusion!' she explained. 'That's what the Doctor calls it. And since he owns it he must know what he's talking about.'

'I ... I suppose so,' Manyak replied, weakly. 'And these instruments, these machines ...?'

'Oh, don't ask me about them. He controls them ... and in a way that only he knows about! It's just double-Dutch to me.' She checked her list again. 'Well, that's it. The lot. So let's take it to the Doctor.'

Manyak nodded and gave her a hand in carrying the items. But before he left he turned back to take one final look round the TARDIS, slowly shaking his head in despair.

A Guardian was stalking a deer. It had been grazing in the open, but as the Guardian closed in on it, it moved under the cover of some trees. The Guardian followed it, stooping low so as not to startle it. Hearing a slight movement overhead, he glanced up. As he did so a fully grown boa constrictor dropped from the overhanging branches and, in a quick movement, wrapped itself around the Guardian, its muscles tightening as he cried out and attempted to shake himself free.

To no avail. The grip was vice-like and the Guardian's flailing arms and legs could find no escape. In mounting terror he cried out again and, after a moment, the Monoid who had accompanied him shuffled up and stood transfixed, staring as the Guardian struggled futilely in the grip of the reptile.

'Help me! For pity's sake, help me!'

The reptilian Monoid seemed fascinated by the action of the boa constrictor. By its scaly skin that was so much like its own, by its obvious strength, and by its aggressiveness.

Then, as the Guardian writhed and was brought to the ground, the Monoid stepped forward, reached out and touched the snake's head. It started to stroke it, gently, moving its own scaled hands along the body, back and forth, caressing it. After a few moments the boa constrictor eased its fierce grip on the Guardian as though having picked up a message from one of its own kind.

The Guardian felt the grip on his body relaxing and, as soon as he could do so, he pulled himself free and swiftly crawled away out of reach of the snake. He lay on the ground, breathing in great gulps of air. Then, as his senses returned and with them a feeling of safety, he watched, fascinated, as the Monoid continued to stroke and soothe the boa constrictor. After a moment the snake started to weave away, finally returning to the tree and climbing it, its tongue flicking in and out as it disappeared from view.

The Monoid walked over to where the Guardian lay on the ground. He reached out his hand to help the man to his feet, but for a moment the Guardian resisted the offer, staring guardedly at the Monoid. Again the Monoid thrust his hand forward. This time the man accepted the offer.

'Thank you,' he said.

The Monoid bowed, then pointed to the deer, which was now grazing a short distance away. The man nodded and they both closed in to capture it.

*

56

The Doctor was in his element, organising his research clinic. Machines to weigh and evaluate, to grind and mix, had been lined up in a factory-like assembly within a long room. On the Doctor's instructions the whole area, already impeccably clean, had now been sterilised by the use of sharply directed steam jets.

'Primitive,' he observed. 'Going back into medical history ... but it will have to do for our immediate purposes.' He picked up some phials that had already been prepared. 'Oh, I know I'm something of an old quack, but the combination of these samples, together with some plant extracts, a little at a time, should do the trick.' He glanced at Rhos. 'But might I be given a look at the medical record of one of you?'

'Why?'

'To find out if any changes have taken place in the human body in ten million years.'

'Oh, yes, of course,' Rhos agreed. 'As a matter of fact I had thought of that too. So I've prepared this scan summary of a body for your observations.'

He beckoned to the Doctor to follow him and led him to a monitor screeen. He pressed an operating key and a body appeared. Then with further flicks of the keys layers were peeled from the example, revealing the inner workings of the Guardians' bodies.

The Doctor stared at the images thoughtfully, muttering his immediate impressions. 'As I rather suspected; the musculature is greatly reduced. Enough to motivate the body ... walking and so on ... but not enough left for any kind of heavy work.'

'Well, for us, that's a thing of the distant past,' Rhos observed.

'Yes, of course. Everything done with the mind.' He glanced at a nearby Monoid. 'And if there is anything physically demanding to be done, then you have the Monoids.'

'True,' Rhos admitted. 'But they seem to enjoy using their talents on manual tasks.'

The Doctor nodded, then stared intently at the screen.

'What's that?' he asked. 'I can see one heart on the left side where it should be – but there seems to be something like it on the other side.'

'It's the second heart,' Rhos stated in a matter-of-fact tone.

'Second?'

'Genetically introduced many Segments ago. In case of malfunction to the first one.' He shrugged. 'Several vital organs have been duplicated for the same reason.'

'H'm! I suppose it makes sense,' said the Doctor. 'But at the same time I notice that other things seem to have disappeared. The vermiform appendix, for example. Where is that?'

'Appendix ...?' Rhos shook his head.

'I see. Genetically removed so long ago that you don't even remember it ... along with the tonsils and other things.' He studied the screen intently. 'I have to take all this into account when it comes to practising my treatment.' He nodded toward the Monoids. 'I take it that you have similar charts of them?'

'Yes,' Rhos replied. He pressed another key and a similar detailed chart of the Monoids' anatomy was revealed on the screen.

'Ah,' the Doctor mused, studying the display. 'Interesting. But wait a minute. Unlike you ... us ... they seem to have no heart at all.'

'No. Instead they have several major pulses – here, here and there.'

'They react to nerve stress?'

'Yes.'

'Ah! So at least they have a nervous system.' He glanced at Rhos. 'The chances are that the treatment will help cure them as well as the Guardians.' He moved away from the monitor screen. 'Now let's get back to work!'

He picked up a phial and poured part of its contents into a measuring jar. 'Now that's the animal compound I have produced, but where is the plant extract, h'm?' As he looked around in search of it a Monoid located it and passed it to him.

'Oh, thank you.' He smiled at the Monoid. 'Very kind of you.'

The Monoid bowed and continued with his work.

The Doctor turned to Rhos, addressing him quietly: 'You know, those Monoids are very intelligent. Much more so than they appear to be at first sight.'

Rhos shrugged and then watched carefully as the Doctor mixed the two compounds together.

In the jail-room, Dodo was nursing Steven when the Doctor bustled in through the open door, carrying a phial containing the mixed compounds.

'Ah, my dear Dodo, how is he?' the Doctor asked.

'Still feverish,' she replied. 'I took his temperature. It's one hundred and two degrees. That's four more than it should be.'

'I'm aware of that!' replied the Doctor testily. 'But let's see what a drop of this nectar does for him.'

He poured some of the compound onto a pad.

'Aren't you going to inject him?' Dodo asked.

'No need for that. No need to make a nasty hypodermic puncture. Just apply this pad – a device I borrowed from that chap Rhos – and the compound will be absorbed into the system through the skin.'

He placed the pad on Steven's arm, then sat alongside him, reading his pulse. 'You know, the Guardians are a somewhat changed species from the likes of yourself and Steven here.'

'But not from you?'

'I've had more experience of adapting,' he replied. 'For instance, they have a greater brain size, two hearts, two livers ... and a greatly reduced intestinal system. That must be because of their changed diet.' He paused in concentration as he felt a tremor in Steven's pulse. 'And as for the Monoids ... well, I know you're not too keen on them ... but even their brain is larger than yours.'

'Those things! Blimey! The next thing you'll tell me is that they can do crosswords and play chess and all sorts of things!'

'It wouldn't surprise me one bit, my dear.' He looked at her searchingly. 'Can you?'

'Well ... er ... I have played cards sometimes ...'

Steven moaned and tossed about on the bench. He seemed to be in some distress and the Doctor looked worried. 'His pulse rate has shot up ... pass me the thermometer. Quickly, girl!'

Dodo did as she was asked. The Doctor placed it under Steven's tongue and held it there for several moments, then withdrew it. He studied the reading with apprehension.

'One hundred and five!' he exclaimed. 'Dangerously high!' He stood up. 'Probably the animal content of that compound is too high. I'll have to adjust it at once.' He hastened away. 'Keep an eye on him!'

'But does that mean that he might die?' Dodo cried in alarm. But the Doctor was gone. She turned to Steven, her face pale and drawn.

The Doctor hurried back into the clinic to face Rhos.

'That first batch was too strong,' he told the microbiologist. 'We'll have to mix another one.'

A Monoid tapped him on the shoulder and passed him a phial. At the same time the Monoid spoke to Rhos in sign language while the Doctor looked on.

'What is it?' he asked. 'What does he say?'

'The Monoid has followed your research technique with interest. He says that he made several different concentrates, and that this phial is a weaker one, with a lower animal content.'

The Doctor was amazed. He held the phial up to the light and shook it. 'Why, yes, I think it is. I can see the difference.' He smiled at the Monoid. 'Thank you, my dear fellow ... thank you, indeed!'

He bustled back out of the clinic while the Monoid bowed in his wake.

*

Back in the jail-room the Doctor hastily used a fresh pad to apply the new dose of vaccine to Steven's arm.

'Any change in temperature?' he asked.

'One hundred and six,' Dodo replied.

'Then let's see what this does.' The Doctor took Steven's wrist and felt for the pulse. 'Racing away!' He continued checking it for several minutes, then glanced up. 'But wait a moment! It seems to be steadying. Check the temperature again.'

Dodo did so ... and smiled.

'It's dropped!' she proclaimed. 'It's down to one hundred and three!'

The Doctor bounced to his feet. 'Then that seems to be the right formula. I must get some of it to the Commander and the others.'

'But isn't it a bit soon to be trying it on them?'

'No! Time is of the essence in a crisis of this sort. And thanks to that clever Monoid I think we've made an important break-through.'

'Clever Monoid ... ?'

'Yes!' He paused for one moment. 'And I'll wager that he'd beat you hands down in a straight game of cards, my dear Dodo.'

He hurried out, leaving Dodo staring after him speechlessly. Then she sighed and turned her attention back to Steven, who by now seemed much calmer as he rested quietly.

The Doctor applied the same remedy to the Commander while Mellium, Rhos and a Monoid looked on.

'This may take a while,' said the Doctor. 'But it's already proving effective with that young companion of mine.'

'But you've already said that he has defensive antibodies in his system to help him,' Rhos observed. 'Whereas the Commander has none.'

'All that may mean is that the treatment may take longer to

realise its full effect,' the Doctor replied. 'But I am hoping that the eventual outcome will be the same.'

'I'm sure that you're right,' Mellium stated. 'Somehow I have faith in you, Doctor.'

'Thank you. No doctor could ask for more.' Automatically he reached for the Commander's wrist, then paused to glance at Rhos. 'Just one main pulse in the wrist?' he asked.

'That's right,' Rhos nodded.

The Doctor made a note of his findings, then invited Rhos to check.

'A little better, I think,' he said. 'Do you agree?'

Rhos concentrated for a moment, then nodded his head. 'Yes, I agree.'

'Good! Then let's make our rounds of the other patients,' the Doctor suggested. 'Lots of work to do, very little time to do it in.' He started out, Rhos following, then paused to address Mellium. 'But still keep your father warm, my dear. Warm and comfy!'

Mellium nodded. 'I will.'

As they made their way along a corridor, Rhos addressed the Doctor.

'How long do you think it will take?' he asked.

The Doctor shook his head uncertainly. 'No way of telling ... not for sure.'

'I hope for your sake – for all our sakes – that it is proved quickly. Zentos is poised like a vulture, ready to swoop if the treatment doesn't work.'

The Doctor sighed, then perked up as they entered a large room that had been converted into a ward.

'Ah! Good morning, everyone!' he announced in his best bedside manner. 'Or afternoon ... or evening ... or whatever! Ready for our treatment, are we?' The rows of patients stared back at him in some amazement. He glanced around. 'Well, where's the ward sister, then?'

'Ward sister?' Rhos asked, uncertainly.

'Yes!' Then the Doctor shrugged. 'But never mind. Let's get on with things as best we can.'

He and Rhos went over to the first patient.

Zentos was pacing up and down near the main panels in the Control Room. He paused to address Manyak, who was in the Commander's seat.

'What are our course readings?' he asked.

'Firmly on path according to the Main Edicts. We should not have to make a course correction for at least a hundred years.'

Zentos smiled thinly. 'Any decision on that will have to be made by our children's children.' Then he frowned. 'That's if there are any.'

'From what I've heard, the treatment prepared by the Doctor is having some good effect.'

'I am still cautious of him and his companions,' Zentos replied. 'They could pull off some kind of temporary trick, just to fool us and put us off our guard.' He paced restlessly. 'Oh, I know you think I'm too distrustful,' he continued. 'But I have to be careful. This mission means everything to me.'

'It does to us all,' Manyak replied quietly.

Zentos glanced at him and paused for a moment.

'Yes, of course,' he agreed, in a suddenly subdued tone. 'I know that, and I am sorry for behaving as though I am the only one who cares.' Then he turned his attention to the Monitor screens. 'Let's see how the treatment is affecting the patients in the main ward.'

Manyak punched up a view of the ward on the screen. It showed the patients lying in rows, apparently quiet, while Guardians and Monoids wearing protective masks moved about, nursing them.

'I fail to see any progress there,' Zentos observed. 'Where is the Doctor now?'

Manyak searched on his bank of screens and then pointed. 'There. In the desert.'

*

The Doctor was riding on a fast moving conveyor across sand dunes, accompanied by Rhos and a Monoid. The Doctor mopped his brow.

'Phew! It's hot here,' the Doctor observed.

'We keep it at the temperature that would have been normal in such a place on Earth,' Rhos replied. 'There isn't much of a population in this area, but there is an important element of animal life.'

In the distance a rising cloud of sand was seen. 'Ah!' said the Doctor. 'Some sign of life over there. A caravan of nomads, by the look of it.'

The Monoid who was driving the conveyor needed no special bidding. He directed the machine so that it veered off in the direction of the desert caravan. The Doctor was intrigued by the fact that their journey to intercept it took longer than he had first estimated, such was the illusion of distance in the desert. But eventually they caught up with it, to find that it was composed of several camels, mounted by Guardians and Monoids.

Greetings were exchanged, then Rhos asked one of the Guardians: 'Are there any sick among you, suffering from the virus disease?'

The Guardian replied: 'Two Guardians there ... and a Monoid at the rear.'

The sick were lying back on improvised stretchers which were pulled by the camels.

The Doctor and Rhos wasted no time. With the aid of the Monoid they set about introducing the vaccine into their systems.

'You had better make camp here,' the Doctor suggested to the Guardian who had spoken with Rhos. 'Rest, and give them a chance for the vaccine to work.'

'A good idea,' the Guardian said. 'Our journey was beginning to tell on us. I've never felt so tired.'

'Perhaps the fever is starting to attack them all!' Rhos suggested.

'Probably! In which case we treat everyone in this caravan,

64

just to make sure.'

The work took some time but eventually all the travellers had been treated. It was only then that the Doctor paused to look around at the desert.

'Ah, beautiful!' he offered his opinion to Rhos. 'Deserts have always been bewitching places, and I must congratulate you and the rest of the Guardians and the Monoids on the way in which you have faithfully recreated the Earth in all its beauty.' Then he glanced off into the distance. 'Even down to the recreation of pyramids!'

In front of the pyramids, a party of Guardians and Monoids were observing the distant caravan and the presence there of the Doctor and Rhos. A Guardian was directing remarks into his wrist communicator.

'The Doctor has administered his treatment to a travelling party in the desert,' he reported.

In the Control Room Zentos listened to this report.

'Thank you,' he replied. 'We have them under scanner surveillance as well.'

Manyak was intrigued by this exchange and its implication. 'Do you mean to say that you have spies following the Doctor and Rhos?' he asked.

'Just part of my security precautions,' Zentos replied. 'In case anything suspicious happens.'

Manyak shook his head in bewilderment.

In the desert the Doctor addressed Rhos. 'But, come!' he said. 'There is still work to be done elsewhere.'

Rhos nodded and moved back to the conveyor. Then the Doctor glanced at the Monoid, who had not stirred. Instead, he was studying a lizard as it basked on a rock in the light, its tongue flicking in and out. The Monoid stared at it with rapt attention; then the Doctor tapped him on the shoulder.

'Time to go,' the Doctor said gently.

The Monoid looked up at him with his swivelling eye, then bowed and moved back to the conveyor. The Doctor stared thoughtfully after him, then looked back at the lizard, marvelling at the way it remained so still while its eyes swivelled, like the Monoid's, darting back and forth to take in the scene around it. Then he shrugged and turned away to join the others in the conveyor.

They set out once more across the desert.

The Commander stirred in his sleep and opened his eyes. Immediately Mellium spoke to him.

'How do you feel now, Father?'

'A little better, I think,' he replied. 'But thirsty.'

Mellium offered him a cup and he sipped some water, then leaned back.

'That's better,' he said. 'What is happening? Have there been any more deaths?'

'No. The Doctor and Rhos are passing on the same treatment to others that they gave you.'

'Good!' He nodded with satisfaction. 'I'm sure that the Doctor means well and will do everything he can.'

In a farmhouse in the cultivated zone the Doctor and his assistants attended to a Guardian and his wife who had been attacked by the fever.

The Guardian's mother stood in the background, watching their careful ministrations. Then the Doctor stepped back. 'That's all we can do for the moment,' he announced. 'We'll just have to wait a little while and see what happens.'

'In that case, perhaps you would care for refreshments?' the mother suggested.

'That would be welcome!' the Doctor exclaimed. He and the others followed the mother downstairs.

The Doctor looked around. 'Interesting,' he remarked. 'I've been in some farmhouses before, but never one quite like this.'

It was totally functional in design. There were no pictures on the walls, no ornaments anywhere, nothing that gave it life or individuality. It obviously served merely as a shelter for the people who lived there.

The mother served up plates of fruit and glasses of juice. 'Thank you,' the Doctor said. 'I am sure this is very healthy for one.'

While the others remained seated to eat their food, the Doctor wandered out of the living room onto a porch.

Before him stretched rolling agricultural land. In the fields he could see Monoids working, harvesting the ripe crops and planting seeds. The mother joined him on the porch.

'You're the one they call the Doctor, aren't you?'

'I have that singular honour.'

'And you and your companions travelled from the Earth . . . but the Earth of many years ago?'

'Most aboard this spaceship are slow to believe in the fact that we can travel through time,' said the Doctor.

'I am an old woman. I have seen much in my life . . . and I have learned that anything is possible.' Her eyes took on a faraway look as she stood for a while, lost in her memories. 'For the others, my son and his wife and the other young people, there was really no choice. They had no future unless they took the long voyage in this spaceship.'

'And you? Did you have a choice?'

'Oh, yes. Many of my generation chose to stay on Earth and take their chance, living out their lives in the place where they had always been.'

'Do you regret leaving?' the Doctor asked her.

'This is an artificial place,' she reflected. 'Oh, it has its purpose . . . but everything about it is manmade. Nothing . . . natural.' She sighed. 'The real Earth is coming to an end . . . but at least it was an Earth one could smell and feel and touch, knowing it had a real history.'

'Where did you live on Earth? In what country?'

'Oh, we didn't have separate names for any part of it,' the

mother replied. 'Those went out a long time ago. But I lived in farmland where there were mountains behind us and a large ocean in front.'

'It sounds attractive.'

'It was the place where I was born and grew up. And the place where I was married.' She sighed. 'But my husband died and that's why I felt that I didn't want to go on living there any more.'

'What did your husband do?'

'He was a farmer like myself. He came from the other side of those mountains to court me, giving up the lands that belonged to his family. Now he is buried in the field behind our old farmhouse there.' She looked around. 'You won't tell the others that I told you that, will you?'

'Of course not ... but why not, especially?'

'Because burial had been prohibited by Earth Law for many Segments. Only cremation was allowed; but I chose to bury my man when he died. I ... I considered it my right.'

'Of course it was,' the Doctor said soothingly. 'So you had many happy times; you, your husband and your family?'

'Yes. Times that I will always remember.'

'You sound very contented,' the Doctor mused. 'You know, the more I've wandered around and observed advanced civilisations, the more I've noticed how unhappy they seem when compared to the old. In your case, much of your happiness must have been due to that place where you worked, ate, slept and played?'

'Yes! Played! Here we don't play. Oh, I suppose the ones who are working on building that statue have something of that feeling ... but for the rest of us, that experience is completely missing.'

The Doctor looked out at the lands. 'The Monoids seem to share a work ethic. But why is it that I can only see them in the fields? No Guardians?'

'Guardians do not like manual labour; Monoids accept it.'

The Doctor's attention was caught by a movement in the distance, among trees. An impression of a mixed party of

Guardians and Monoids. They seemed to be interested in the farmhouse and his presence there. Then he shrugged, dismissing the thought.

Rhos called from within: 'Everything is all right!'

A quick examination of the patients proved this to be true. 'That's it!' the Doctor exclaimed. 'This vaccine is successful, no matter what the climate!'

They left the patients with the Doctor giving the mother final advice: 'Warm and comfy! That's the way they should be kept and they'll be back to normal in a few days!'

'Thank you, Doctor,' the mother said. She touched his arm and delayed him for a moment while Rhos and the Monoid walked out to the conveyor. 'I have this which I brought from Earth. So it's real. Now, take a piece and I will hold on to the rest to remind me of my old home.'

The Doctor took it and nodded understandingly, then left the house. As he climbed into the conveyor Rhos asked him: 'What have you got there?'

'A sprig of heather,' the Doctor replied.

Zentos had received the report about the Doctor and his movements in the cultivated zone and pursed his lips as he wondered where he might go next.

The polar bear reared on its hind legs, threatening the Doctor, Rhos and the Monoid as they hove into view in the icy regions of the polar cap.

'Good heavens!' the Doctor exclaimed. 'What a powerful-looking beast!'

'And still a dangerous one,' Rhos replied. 'One of the species that failed to respond to our genetic treatments of many Segments ago.'

'Then I suggest that we give it a wide berth,' the Doctor said firmly. In answer the Monoid guided the conveyor away from the area of danger. The Doctor shivered.

'After the other places this is quite a contrast. Cold! But on the other hand it's a dry cold. It's doubtful if the virus would have reached anyone in this area.'

'We'll soon find out,' Rhos replied. 'There's a settlement over there.' He indicated a cluster of low buildings.

But the Doctor's prediction was proved wrong the moment they entered the buildings. Everyone inside, Guardians and Monoids, was laid low by the fever. They were lying in their beds and some were huddled on the floor.

The Doctor surveyed the scene in dismay.

'So I was wrong. And in these climatic conditions the fever will have a sharper effect.'

Rhos had quickly moved among the stricken victims, checking each in turn as did the Doctor and the Monoid. From a corner he called out: 'You're right! There are two here who are dead.'

The Doctor glanced over and saw that Rhos was pointing at the bodies of a Guardian and a Monoid. 'Yes,' he observed, 'And the rest of them are so ill that they have obviously not been able to bury them. The first thing we must do is get those bodies outside.'

He and the others hastily donned their protective masks. Now they worked together to move the dead bodies out into the snow. There they started covering the cadavers with snow, swiftly forming makeshift graves.

From a high mound in the distance their actions were observed by the party of Guardians and Monoids that Zentos had instructed to follow them. Immediately they reported what they saw back to him.

Zentos listened to the report in the Control Room and clipped his fingers impatiently.

'More dead!' he informed Manyak. 'And Rhos seems to be working along with the Doctor to conceal them! Which means that I was right to keep an eye on events.'

*

Once back in the buildings, the Doctor, Rhos and the Monoid started on the task of helping the other patients.

'I suppose by rights we should have a stronger vaccine,' the Doctor reflected. 'But that would take time, going back to the clinic and then returning here. Instead, I suggest we give them a first treatment of the one we have, monitor them and then, if necessary, give them a booster treatment.'

They worked diligently, moving among the patients and administering the first shots of the vaccine. The Doctor made up a chart on which he noted down each of the building's occupants by a number and then recorded their temperature and pulse rate readings.

Eventually they had applied the first dose of the treatment. The Doctor leaned back and addressed Rhos and the Monoid.

'Well, that's that! Our first step. Now all we can do is wait and see what happens.'

Zentos strode through the Great Hall, passing the work in progress on the Homo Sapiens statue without a glance. He made his way along a corridor and entered a room.

In it were a number of Guardians and Monoids. They were clothed in special, distinctive uniforms.

Zentos addressed them: 'Your attention, please! As you know, I have organised you as a security force in the event that anything should go wrong. Well, now it has. More deaths have occurred.' There was a murmur of consternation and anger. 'So now you must arrest the intruders and we will have to carry out the original sentence of expelling them into outer space!'

They nodded in agreement. One Guardian asked, 'But where are they?'

'The two young ones are in the room where we first placed them. And the Doctor is with microbiologist Rhos in the polar regions at the co-ordinates of KZ8 and WN3.'

They prepared to set out, but Zentos delayed them. 'And when you arrest the Doctor, bring in Rhos as well. There is some indication that he may have fallen under the spell of the Doctor and may be a traitor, so we need him for questioning!'

Nodding, they set out on their mission.

The Doctor examined several of the patients in the polar buildings, while Rhos attended to others.

'There seems to be some improvement,' the Doctor stated. 'What about those you've examined?'

'A little,' Rhos concurred.

'But not as much as we could have hoped for,' the Doctor concluded. 'So let's give them another dose of the treatment. We might get better results then.'

They set about the task immediately, the Doctor deciding on the dosages to be given after consulting the notes he had made on his first examination of the patients. They had varied in their reactions to the first stage of the treatment; some required a full second vaccination, others only milder doses. The Doctor was well aware that his judgements were entirely subjective, but in these special circumstances he had only his instinct to guide him.

Rhos had recognised this, too; and so had the Monoid. But their respect for the Doctor had gradually grown as they had wandered around the hinterland of the Ark, and they faithfully followed his every instruction.

When the police Guardians and Monoids entered the jail-room in which the intruders had first been incarcerated and where Steven had been nursed by Dodo, they were greeted by the sight of Steven standing on his feet, Dodo at his side.

'What's this?' Steven asked.

'We have instructions to take you back into custody,' a Guardian stated.

'Why?' Dodo asked.

'Because there have been more deaths from the fever you brought to this space ship.'

72

'But look at him,' Dodo argued. 'Steven was as sick as anyone, but now he's cured!'

The Guardian could see that this was true, but he shook his head. 'It makes no difference. We have our instructions, so you will come with us.'

Steven sighed. 'We'll have to go, Dodo.'

'I suppose so,' she said sulkily. 'But wait until the Doctor hears about this. He'll flip his lid!'

'The Doctor is being sought now,' the Guardian informed them. 'Then we will find out what ... er ... "flipping his lid" means.'

At first they were dark dots, moving through the snowy wastes of the polar region.

It was the Monoid who had noticed them when he had glanced out of the buildings at the surrounding landscape. He indicated them to the Doctor and Rhos.

'Animals?' the Doctor asked.

'Yes,' Rhos had answered. 'Of our kind.'

It was true, for as the dots came close and took on recognisable shape, they were revealed as Guardians and Monoids.

'Strange,' the Doctor observed. 'I wouldn't have thought you would have had so many in this region.'

'Normally we don't. But these are Guardians and Monoids with a special task, judging by the uniform they are wearing.'

The Doctor pursed his lips, guessing instantly what Rhos was implying. 'Then let's check on these patients and see how they're doing, before anything untoward happens.'

Quickly he, Rhos and the Monoid did so, moving from one individual to another, taking their temperatures and pulse rates and reacting in pleased surprise as they found them to be returning to normal. At the same time the patients were coming to and starting to talk coherently between themselves.

'Splendid!' the Doctor cried. 'We've made progress, after all!'

Then he and the others glanced around as the doors of the building were flung open and the police party of Guardians and Monoids entered.

'Ah!' the Doctor exclaimed by way of greeting. 'So glad to see you ... and to inform you that these fellows, who were all sick, are now making excellent progress!'

'You will come with us, Doctor,' the leading Guardian ordered. 'You are under arrest.' He turned to the microbiologist. 'You, too, Rhos!'

'Arrest?' the Doctor protested. 'But surely there must be some mistake?'

'None!' the Guardian replied. 'Orders!'

'But ...' the Doctor looked around hopelessly, '... what about these patients? We have treated them, but they still need nursing.'

The Guardian gestured toward the Monoid who had accompanied the Doctor and Rhos. 'He can take care of them.'

The Doctor sighed. 'Ah, yes, if you say so.' He went over to the Monoid. 'I think by now you know what is to be done, old chap.' The Monoid nodded. 'If there are any more attacks or resistance by the virus, treat them with the vaccine. And above all, continue to make sure that they are kept warm.' He patted the Monoid's shoulder in encouragement, then turned to the arresting Guardian. 'Now, just who is it who has ordered our arrest ... and why?'

'It is on my instructions that you have been brought here,' Zentos stated as he addressed the Doctor and his companions, together with Rhos, in front of an assembly of Guardians and Monoids. 'We have learnt of more deaths, this time in the polar region. And you, Doctor, were seen organising the hiding of the bodies.'

'Stuff and nonsense!' the Doctor exploded.

Dodo turned to the Guardian who had arrested her and Steven. 'That's what's meant by "flipping his lid"!' she said.

'We weren't hiding the bodies,' the Doctor explained. 'We were just giving them a temporary burial. Isn't that so, Rhos?'

'Yes,' Rhos replied.

'They had already been dead for some time when we found them,' the Doctor continued. 'And the rest of their friends in that polar station were sick and unable to carry out the task. But now, thanks to our treatment, they are recovering!'

'All I know is that there were deaths. So far only your own kind,' Zentos indicated Steven and Dodo 'seem to be fully recovered. I still believe that you are a threat, and that the original sentence of expelling you into space should be carried out!' He turned to face the assembled Guardians and Monoids. 'What do you say now? No Guardian or Monoid has yet achieved full recovery, so should we execute that sentence?'

There was a mixed reaction. Some were for carrying out the sentence, others were more restrained.

Zentos grew impatient. 'And while we are at it, the fate of microbiologist Rhos should also be decided, for he seems to have thrown in his lot with the Doctor without caution. He even helped to hide the bodies of the dead.'

This brought a firmer response from the assembly. There were cries of: 'Carry out the sentence!' 'Expel them!' 'And with them, the traitor!'

'Very well, then,' barked Zentos. 'Take them away and carry out the sentence.'

As the Doctor and his companions, together with Rhos, were seized and led away protesting, Mellium entered the control room and addressed them: 'My father ...'

'What about him?' Zentos asked.

'He wishes to speak to you!'

Automatically Zentos and the others glanced at the relay source. Zentos addressed it: 'Yes, Commander?'

'You are making a foolish and unjust mistake!' the Commander declared.

But his voice did not come from the relay source. Instead it came directly from the Commander himself as he strode into the Control Room.

'For as you can see, I am well... totally restored to health!' He smiled at the Doctor. 'Thanks to the skills of our visitors!'

There was immediate consternation among the Guardians and the Monoids, who automatically released their captives.

'My fever has totally abated,' the Commander stated emphatically. 'My temperature is back to normal and my pulse is regular.' He turned to Zentos. 'I think that you are making a hasty judgement, Zentos. I respect your reasons, but I am compelled to over-rule you.'

'Thank heavens for that,' Dodo ejaculated. 'I like space travel, but not the sort of journey they were planning for us!'

The Doctor smiled. 'For once your English seems to be in order and expresses my feelings exactly.'

Zentos finally spoke: 'I am glad to see that you are well, Commander; but I must make sure of the others.'

He signalled to Manyak to make a monitor scan of the distant places that the Doctor and Rhos had visited. The images came in quickly and from all points the evidence was the same. All those who had been struck down by the fever were now fully recovered. Zentos turned to the Doctor.

'It seems that I owe you a deep apology, Doctor. You and your companions.'

'Think nothing of it, dear boy,' the Doctor replied magnanimously. 'Everyone can make a mistake. We made ours by bringing the fever here in the first place ...'

'And put it right by curing it,' Zentos stated.

Manyak suddenly attracted their attention by referring to the master monitor screen. 'Look at this,' he called. 'The Earth ...'

They all stared in fascinated horror at the monitor screen as the Earth could be seen finally tumbling out of its normal orbit around the Sun. It hurtled towards it, first its fringes catching fire, then the whole planet transformed into a ball of flame.

'The last moments for Earth have arrived,' the Doctor pronounced. He turned to the Guardians and the Monoids.

'Let's hope that your Refusis turns out to be just as agreeable a place as the Earth once was.'

He made his way into the Great Hall, followed by Steven, Dodo, the Commander and the others.

'That's something we will never know, Doctor,' the Commander replied. 'Only our descendants will find that out.'

'In seven hundred years,' said Dodo. 'And by that time that thing will be finished.'

She pointed to the statue of Homo Sapiens. So far only the feet and one of its ankles had taken shape.

'That ... er ... thing is a symbol of hope, my dear,' the Doctor pointed out. Then he turned to the Commander and the others. 'Well, goodbye, my friends. And my best wishes for your journey!'

He and his companions shook hands with them all. And the Doctor, reaching the end of the line, surprised a Monoid by shaking hands with him also.

The creature stared back at him with his one, swivelling eye. Then he quietly returned the handshake ... and this time did not bow, as was his custom.

Instead, he indicated to his fellow Monoids that they should accompany the Doctor. He, Steven and Dodo were driven out of the Great Hall on a conveyor, waving goodbye as they went.

The conveyor deposited the Doctor and his companions in the glade alongside the TARDIS. There were final goodbyes all round, then Dodo paused for a moment and looked around the jungle.

'This place,' she mused. 'It gave us a dodgy moment or so ... but now that we're leaving, I'll miss it.'

'Come on, my dear,' the Doctor urged. 'We're travellers ... not settlers!' He addressed Steven. 'Get the main booster started,' he commanded. 'At least, I've taught you how to do that.'

'Yes, Doctor,' Steven replied. He entered the TARDIS, followed by Dodo.

The Doctor himself appeared loath to leave this green and pleasant spaceship ... especially when he thought of the comparatively bumpy ride to follow in his old TARDIS. But then he shrugged, gave the Monoids on the conveyor a final wave ... and followed his companions into the craft.

A few moments later the engines could be heard whining and revving up ... then, quite suddenly and to the astonishment of the watching Monoids, the TARDIS disappeared ... leaving the Ark behind.

5

The Return

In the TARDIS, as it journeyed through the cosmos, Dodo was asleep and the Doctor muffled a yawn.

'Must get some rest myself,' he mumbled to Steven. 'So that will leave you in charge. Now, I've shown you all the main controls. Keep an eye on them, dear boy; and if anything unusual happens, call me immediately.'

'Yes, Doctor,' Steven agreed.

The Doctor settled himself down in a seat, allowing his head to drop back as he dozed off. Steven marvelled at the seemingly non-stop energy of the Doctor; he knew that the so-called 'rest' would amount to no more than a cat-nap. It was in this way that the Doctor kept going, whereas he and Dodo required several hours' sleep in every twenty-four. Thinking about this, he yawned as he glanced at the main control instruments.

Their readings were steady. For a moment he wondered where they might be heading now . . . and in which time span. Then the instruments blurred out of focus as he once again muffled a yawn.

It would be his turn to sleep properly when the Doctor and Dodo returned to duty, but Steven was having trouble in staving off the feeling of fatigue that was engulfing him. Maybe the after-effects of that fever he had experienced on the Ark, he thought; but no, that must be a long way back now, and the TARDIS and the Ark were travelling apart, putting time and distance between them.

It was no good, Steven just had to sit down. He could just as easily watch the instruments from a sitting position and there was no sense in inviting a chance relapse.

As he seated himself, he failed to notice that his sleeve had caught the lever of one of the main instruments and altered its position.

'Wake up!' the Doctor snapped.

Steven jerked to full consciousness to find the irate Doctor and Dodo standing over him.

'Oh ... sorry, but I must have dozed off,' Steven said.

'Dozed?' the Doctor demanded. He glanced impatiently at the instruments. 'According to these we've wandered off any kind of target. Heaven knows where we are now!' He studied the Main Indicator. 'And according to this we're about to make a landing!'

Dodo peered over his shoulder. 'Any idea where, Doctor?'

'No! Thanks to Steven here we've completely lost track.'

'Sorry, Doctor,' Steven mumbled.

The Doctor relented. 'Don't worry about it, my dear boy. Perhaps it's my fault, asking you to do too much, too soon.'

There was a shivering motion throughout the TARDIS.

'Hang on!' the Doctor cried out. 'It *is* a landing!'

Dodo grabbed a console. 'I've never liked this part! We always assume that we're going to come down on land, but what happens if we end up in the middle of some flipping ocean?'

The Doctor glared at her impatiently. 'Then we get wet, my dear. Very wet indeed!'

Then the grinding and winding and whirl of machinery ceased as the TARDIS settled down. The Doctor looked again uncertainly at his instruments ... then reached forward and operated the exit door lever.

It swung open and Dodo moved toward it. The Doctor caught her sleeve and held her back.

'Not so fast, my dear,' he said. 'I'll go first; you two follow me after I've had a chance to look around.'

The Doctor emerged from the TARDIS ... and looked around in amazement. He called back: 'Come on out here, both of you!'

Doctor and Dodo did so ... and, in turn, cried out in

astonishment when they saw where they were.

'But it can't be ...' Steven ejaculated.

'Too fantastic to be true!' Dodo exclaimed.

'But that's it!' the Doctor answered. 'Fantastic but true!'

They were back in the jungle glade aboard the Ark!

They had made a hurried survey of their surroundings.

'The same place – the *exact* same place,' the Doctor observed.

'But that can't be,' Dodo said. 'We've only been gone a short time.'

'Time is only relative, my dear,' the Doctor rejoined. 'I've always told you that.' He glanced around. 'It *is* the same place ... but there are things about it that are different.'

'What, for instance?' Steven asked.

'The trees ... the foliage ... most things look the same,' the Doctor mused. 'Yet there is a difference about the flora that puzzles me.'

Dodo cupped her hands to her mouth and called out: 'Guardians! Monoids! We're back!'

There was no reply.

'Let's go to the city,' Steven suggested. 'Maybe we can find them there!'

'Er ... yes,' the Doctor agreed cautiously. 'No harm in that, I suppose.'

But there was the threat of harm as they moved through the jungle on their way to the city.

All around them they could hear the animals stirring, howling and crying out in a way that they had not done previously. Ahead of them they saw a tiger tracking a gazelle, but this time behaving as it has done in ages past on Earth. The gazelle was grazing, but pricked up its ears when it sensed danger ... and took off in flight as the tiger closed in on it. There was a brief skirmish, raising a cloud of dust, as the tiger pounced on the gazelle and killed it. They froze in horror on seeing this.

'That's not the way that other tiger behaved,' Dodo finally said.

'No,' said the Doctor. 'So, as far as the animals are concerned, we had better not trust them.'

They continued on their way, eventually reaching the safety of the city.

Within, in the vast corridors that led to the centre of the city, they sensed that things were not as they had been.

'Where's everyone?' Steven queried.

'Maybe it's some kind of galactic holiday,' Dodo suggested without conviction.

The Doctor was thoughtful as he continued walking forward, glancing right and left. Finally he led them into the Great Hall.

Again, no sign of life, either on the Hall floor or on the galleries that surrounded it. The Doctor paused, deep in thought. But then he looked up, startled, as Dodo cried out: 'Doctor ... Steven ... look!' She pointed. 'The statue! They've finished building it!'

All three stared at it.

It stood there, dominating the Great Hall as it was meant to do. Towering over them. Looking roughly like the plan they had originally been shown.

But there was a vital difference and Steven was the first to notice it. 'It wasn't meant to look like that ...'

'What do you mean?' asked the Doctor.

'... it was meant to represent Homo Sapiens ... but that head on top ... it's the head of a Monoid!'

'Good heavens, dear boy, you're right!'

'They must have made some kind of mistake,' Dodo said. 'But *some* mistake! There's a lot of difference between a human head and one of those one-eyed creatures!'

'Yes, my dear,' the Doctor observed, 'but whatever the confusion, one fact remains ...'

'What's that?' Steven asked.

'The statue is finished,' the Doctor replied. 'Which means that seven hundred years have passed since we last stood here!'

'Seven hundred ...' Dodo echoed. Then she shuddered. 'No wonder the place feels so different. Grotty ...' She hesitated as she felt the Doctor glance at her sharply. 'But seven hundred years – that's the time the Guardians estimated that their journey would take them to reach Refusis.'

'Only one place to find out what's happened,' said the Doctor briskly, starting to stride away.

'Where's that?' Steven asked.

'The Control Room.'

The Control Room was deserted when they entered it. The Doctor looked around and, followed by the others, moved over to the central bank of monitor screens.

He studied the flight and guidance controls. 'There have been some changes,' he announced. 'Everything about this Master Deck is automatic now. No hands-on required ... just leave it to the program of the Main Edicts that were laid down at the beginning of the Ark's voyage.'

'Then where is this spaceship now?' Steven asked.

The Doctor had been studying a main screen. 'Close to its target planet,' he stated. 'I think that must be Refusis there.'

He indicated a planet that was looming large on the screen.

'In that case, where are the Guardians?' Dodo asked. 'Well, at least the descendants of the ones that we knew before? Surely they must be around somewhere ...'

The Doctor had been operating the controls on the secondary monitor screens. Familiar scenes appeared: the jungle, the desert, the cultivated lands, the polar regions, and the caverns where the trays were kept, holding in micro-form and in suspension the beings brought from the Earth many decades before.

'Nothing about those places seems to have changed,' Steven observed. 'But there's still no signs of ordinary life.'

'I think that's where you're wrong, my boy,' the Doctor

exclaimed. 'Look at that!'

An image appeared on the screen that showed them the first sign of a Guardian since they had re-entered the Ark.

But there was something different about this man. Instead of moving confidently, he behaved in a near-servile manner as he picked up a flask and a cup and brought them forward to a reptilian hand that reached out to receive the offering of refreshment.

'But that looks like a Monoid!' Steven exclaimed.

'And the Guardian seems to be working for it like some kind of a servant,' Dodo said.

The Doctor had searched among other screens and indicated another image.

'He's not the only one who's doing that!' he said.

On the screen they could see several Guardians at work in a kitchen, preparing food . . . while in the background a Monoid watched their every move.

'The Guardians appear to be slaves!' Steven said.

'Yes!' the Doctor agreed. 'And the Monoids seem to be their overlords!'

As they watched, one of the Guardians accidentally dropped several plates. He bent to pick them up but before he could do so the Monoid raised a weapon and pointed it at him.

There was a sustained flash . . . and the Guardian was extinguished, dissolving to nothing.

'What was that?' gasped Steven in astonishment.

'Some kind of gun,' the Doctor replied. 'Probably based on a laser principle. A Particle Destructor. Very effective . . . and, as you saw, very deadly.'

'What happened to the spaceship of brotherly love?' Dodo demanded. 'Where Guardians and Monoids worked together for one common purpose?'

'Obviously things have changed!' the Doctor mused. Then he glanced up. 'But I think we might get some of the answers now.'

Monoids had entered the Control Room, followed by a couple of subservient Guardians. These Monoids were armed with the same weapons the Doctor and his companions had seen on the monitor; and, in addition to their obvious status as rulers, there were other things that were different about them.

They each wore a collar around their necks and on the collars numbers were stamped, identifying them. But they also used the collar in a special way. It apparently enabled them to speak, albeit in a mechanical, toneless way.

'What are you doing here?' Number Two asked.

'Things have obviously changed,' Steven muttered.

'They can speak now!' Dodo said. 'Something that they couldn't do before.'

'I asked,' Number Two repeated, 'what are you doing here ... and who are you?'

The Doctor replied. 'We are ... visitors ... to this spaceship. On a second visit. We were here many centuries ago. We come as friends.'

'Friends to whom?' Number Two demanded.

'To all who travel in this spaceship.'

'You mean, to the humanoids like yourselves?'

'Well ... er ... yes! But also to yourselves, the Monoids. We were friends of all on our previous visit ...' The Doctor looked appraisingly at the weapon that Number Two was holding. 'But things were very different then.'

'You speak of the distant past,' said Number Two dismissively. 'Following the revolution, we Monoids are now the masters!'

'And the human beings?'

'They work for us.' He turned to face one of the Guardians. 'Is that not so, Yendom?'

Yendom's reply was low and acquiescent. 'Yes. It is true.'

'We conquered ... and they obey,' Number Two stated. 'And so will you ... you strangers who have come into our midst. Now, you will come with us.'

'Where?'

'To our leader, Number One.'

He indicated the door. When the Doctor and the others

hesitated uncertainly, he thrust his weapon forward, threatening them.

The Doctor sighed. 'Might as well do what the chap says,' the told the others. 'Otherwise I have the feeling that the consequences could be ... unfortunate!'

The Doctor led the way, holding himself erect and maintaining what dignity he could. Steven and Dodo followed, their escort party flanking them as they left the Control Room.

Number One was leaning back in a chair as he devoured grapes and drank from a goblet of wine that had been offered to him by his servant, the Guardian Maharis.

'This fruit is excellent and the wine to my taste,' he stated. 'You are a good and obedient servant.'

Maharis bowed. 'I am glad to have the honour to be such, Number One.'

The door to this Main Comfort Chamber slid open and Number Two entered. He addressed his leader. 'Here are the strangers, Number One.'

'Wait!' Number One switched on a monitor. 'Look at this page from history.'

They watched the screen on which the Doctor, Steven and Dodo were seen making their farewells prior to leaving the Ark seven hundred years before. The Doctor could be seen following the others into the TARDIS ... and within moments it dissolved and disappeared as it left the Ark.

All three – Number One, Number Two and Maharis – were fascinated by the way in which the TARDIS had vanished. Then Number One switched off the monitor and motioned to the Doctor and his companions to enter.

'It seems that when you were here before the Guardians of that day didn't believe that you could travel through time as well as space. Why have you come back?' he asked.

Steven shrugged. 'The TARDIS made the decision.'

'Are you telling me that you can't control your own

machine?'

'What's it got to do with you?' Dodo demanded.

'Ssh ... ssh, my child!' the Doctor muttered hastily.

'According to the History Scan you brought a strange fever that killed many of our ancestors,' Number One said accusingly.

'Yes. But we cured it, didn't we?' Dodo rejoined. 'Or at least, the Doctor here did.'

'He thought he did!'

'And what do you mean by that?' the Doctor asked.

'You controlled the immediate impact of the fever,' Number One replied. 'But a mutation of it developed later on that sapped the will of the so-called Guardians.'

'Are you saying that it was our fault that you took over?' Dodo asked. 'Because of that fever?'

'In part ...'

'Were there other reasons?' Steven enquired.

'The main factor was the Guardians themselves. They were simple beings. Too trusting. They actually encouraged the research from which we developed our voice boxes ... and carelessly left open the archive records in which were deposited the designs for these heat weapons. It was simple then for us to make them ... and they were totally unprepared for the conflict when it came.'

'What happened?' Dodo was curious to know.

'Many were killed ... the rest are prisoners. A fact that you will shortly see for yourselves.' He turned in his chair. 'Number Two, take these strangers to the Security Kitchen.'

'Yes, Number One.'

'And when you have done that call a Grand Council meeting of the Monoids up to Number Twenty.'

'It will be done.' Number Two indicated the door to the Doctor and his companions. 'This way,' he commanded.

The Doctor looked for a moment as though he might argue with Number One, but then shrugged and led Steven and Dodo out of the Main Comfort Chamber.

Number One looked at Maharis with his one, swivelling

eye. 'I trust that the visit by these strangers won't give you any strange ideas, Maharis?'

'Er, no, Number One,' Maharis replied. 'I am content to obey the Monoid Order.'

Number One nodded, satisfied with this answer.

In the Security Kitchen a Guardian, Dassuk, whispered to a girl: 'Who told you all this?'

'One of the subject Guardians passed the information on when he passed by the door just now,' Venussa replied.

'Strangers? But what sort of strangers?'

'Human beings!'

'Then I'm afraid the Monoids will make very short work of them.'

'Not so far,' she answered. 'They've been taken prisoner.'

'Well, that proves it's only a rumour! Just like many others that we've heard down through the years. Look, Venussa, you know how far the Ark has travelled ... and how the Monoids made constant searches for our kind after they took over ... so where could these so-called human beings have come from?'

'From Earth!'

'Impossible! The Earth has been destroyed.'

'But they came from it millions of years ago. They've travelled through time ...'

'That isn't possible!' He regarded her sceptically. 'I think you've been a prisoner for far too long!'

'Oh, but it could be true, Dassuk,' Venussa replied. 'Don't you remember the stories about the time when this space voyage was begun? When a Doctor and a young couple came and then went again? Why, they were the first people to call this ship the Ark!'

'That's just a legend. And legends won't help us regain control of the Ark!'

On their escorted journey through the spaceship the Doctor

and his companions had noticed the changed conditions. Now they saw more Monoids, each armed with a weapon similar to the one Number Two carried ... and realised that the Monoids were indeed in total control of the Ark.

A party of captive Guardians shuffled past them, hauling materials in the manner of pack-mules. An armed Monoid followed in their wake.

One of the Guardians stumbled, to be caught by the Doctor.

'Thank you,' the Guardian murmured. Then he looked at the Doctor's clothing in puzzled amazement. 'What ... who are you ...?' he asked.

'I am the Doctor,' came the reply. 'And these are my companions, Steven and Dorothea!'

'Dodo!' she snapped.

'But what part of the Ark do you come from?' the Guardian called back as he stumbled on with his load.

'Stop talking, there!' the Monoid in charge of his party shouted. He, Number Seven, then addressed Number Two. 'What have you got here, Number Two?'

'Strangers!' Number Two replied tersely.

The Doctor and the others were led on beyond the work party they had passed and, in the Great Hall, Number Two called for them to halt for a moment. He pointed upwards.

'You see!' he said. 'That statue is the symbol of our Monoid Order!'

They stared at it, noting the human feet and calves ... and then the scaly arms emerging from its tunic, the whole topped by the one-eyed, mop-thatched head.

'Nonsense!' Dodo snorted. 'You may have taken it over, but you didn't think it up or start it.'

'Don't provoke him,' the Doctor murmured.

The Monoid stared at Dodo, his one eye fixed on her.

'Well ... on second thoughts ... it's not bad!' she said. 'After all, any carnival would love to have it.'

The Monoid gestured to them to keep walking and they filed out of the Great Hall.

The door of the Security Kitchen was opened and the party of captives was ushered inside.

'This way, Doctor,' Number Two said. 'And bring your friends in with you.' He indicated the work tables. 'You will stay in this place and take on the task of preparing our food. You will not leave here. This is where you will work ... and this is where you will sleep, like the others of your kind. Above all, you must always be obedient prisoners!'

The Doctor listened to this with his head cocked slightly. Then he bowed ... and, after a moment, Dodo and Steven followed suit.

'Good. I do not think you will be much trouble ... any more than the others have been.' Number Two seemed satisfied and left the Security Kitchen.

The arrival of the Doctor and his companions had aroused the curiosity of the prisoners working in the kitchen. Venussa left her work place, followed by Dassuk.

'Doctor?' she queried. 'Did he say ... Doctor?'

'Yes, he did.'

'Have you been here before? On the Ark, I mean?'

The Doctor nodded.

'But that's incredible!' Dassuk exclaimed. 'How in space did you do it?'

'If I were to tell you, young man, you wouldn't believe me!' the Doctor informed him.

Steven cut in: 'And besides, we've got far more important things to talk about! We've got to find a way of getting out of this place!'

At the Grand Council Meeting he had convened in a Special Chamber, Number One was addressing Numbers Two to Twenty.

'In a short while, Refusis will be ours. We will land there. And there we will create a Monoid world!'

There was a rumour of approval from the Council. Then Number Four spoke up: 'But, Number One, what about the

90

Guardians?'

'I have a simple plan that will destroy them,' Number One stated. 'When we create our new world on that planet it will be without any memory of – or reference to – the time when we were secondary beings.'

'That's as it should be,' Number Two agreed.

'But at this moment we cannot be sure what Refusis is really like,' Number One continued. 'Or what kind of creatures the Refusians are. So I am sending a forward landing party ahead of us.'

'But in that case the Refusians will be forewarned,' objected Number Two.

'I have thought of that,' Number One replied. 'So I want you to listen to my plan ...'

In the Security Kitchen Dodo was in her element as she talked with the captive Guardians. '*I* was the first one to call this ship the Ark!'

'And when you came here you brought that strange fever ... and the Doctor was the one who cured it,' Dassuk recalled.

'Of course!'

'But that fever – and its consequences – were our undoing.'

Venussa interjected: 'Take no notice of him. Dassuk was born a cynic.'

'Then he'll probably die as one,' the Doctor observed. 'That is, unless we do something quickly about this situation.'

'Are there many other Guardians like yourselves being held prisoner?' Steven asked.

'The majority,' Dassuk replied. 'But on the other hand there are those who have chosen to serve the Monoids. The subservient ones.'

'But why don't we just choose our moment and jump on the Monoids?' Dodo asked. 'Better to die fighting than ...'

'We feel like that sometimes. But you forget that they are armed with the heat guns whereas we are not. And those weapons are lethal.'

'But we could take the chance and try to seize one,' Steven urged. 'Then challenge them at their own game.'

'They are very careful. The Monoids never put them down.'

'But the situation is an urgent one,' the Doctor said. 'Time is running out. Soon the landings will start on the planet Refusis.'

'Fetch the Doctor and the girl who came with him,' Number One instructed Number Two.

'Yes, Number One,' Number Two replied.

He moved out of the Council Chamber while Number One addressed the other Monoids.

'Their presence here is something that we can turn to our own advantage. They will act as our shield in our first probes on the strange planet. And if they are injured or destroyed in the attempt that will help save Monoid lives!'

'Do you think you can make this attempt?' Dodo asked.

'We must try,' Dassuk answered. 'Otherwise there will be no future for us. And our forefathers might just as well have stayed on the Earth and died with it.'

Venussa had been listening near the door. 'They are coming back!' she hissed urgently.

They hastily spread themselves out, taking up planned positions. The door slid open and an armed Monoid entered. He looked around and demanded, 'Why aren't you working?'

Venussa caught a nodded signal from Steven and purposely tipped a plate onto the floor, where it clattered loudly. The Monoid turned to look at it and Steven called out, 'Now!'

He and several others tackled the Monoid from behind, quickly pinning back his arms. At the same time Dassuk wrested the weapon from the Monoid's grasp, but in the skirmish was unable to hold onto it. It fell to the floor.

The door slid open again and another Monoid, Number

Two, entered. He took in the situation at a glance and exclaimed, 'What is this!?'

A young Guardian hastily reached for the weapon that lay on the floor. Immediately Number Two levelled his own weapon at him. There was a blast ... and the young Guardian was exterminated.

Number Two covered the rest of them with his lethal weapon. Dassuk, Steven and the others recognised that their action had failed and released the Monoid they were holding. He immediately picked up the heat gun that had been wrested from him.

Number Two addressed them. 'You are reckless and stupid. Now you have achieved only one thing – the death of another of your kind.' He faced the Doctor. 'Doctor, you and that girl there' he indicated Dodo 'will come with me!'

The Doctor sighed and started out through the open door, followed by Dodo who looked apprehensively at the scaly creature who was giving the orders. Steven started to follow, but Number Two stayed his move with a wave of his arm.

'You will stay here!' he ordered.

'Why?' Steven demanded. 'Where are you taking them?'

'They will make the first landing on the planet Refusis. You will be held as a security for their conduct.'

Steven fell back, defeated, as the door slid shut.

In the area of the Launch Bays Monoids bustled around as they prepared a vehicle for departure. A Monoid spoke into his wrist communicator.

'The Launch Ship is ready, Number One. Number Nine, the Doctor, the girl and the Guardian called Yendom are aboard.'

The reply came back from Number One. 'Good! Then let's hope that they succeed in their mission.'

The ejection energy was activated and the Launcher left the chamber in which it had been placed, speeding away from the Ark.

Within the Launcher, the Doctor was aware that it was travelling at a great speed. So fast that there was hardly any feeling of motion.

He looked round at the others in the craft. Dodo appeared apprehensive, the Guardian, obviously a subservient one, stared blankly at the walls of the Launcher, and Number Nine seemed unperturbed as he manned the controls.

A jolly party, the Doctor thought to himself, to go venturing into the unknown. But then his thoughts were interrupted as the Launcher began to slow down and finally made a landing. The Monoid operated the release lever of the door and they rose to their feet and stepped out of the Launcher.

They stood, grouped together, gazing about them. They had arrived. This, at last, was the planet Refusis.

6

Refusis

Trees . . . shrubbery . . . fields. The Doctor recognised that the First Guardian Commander had been right when he had stated, those seven hundred years before, that this planet Refusis was like Earth.

It was – and at the same time, it wasn't. It had the same physical characteristics, but there was an important element that was missing. There was no sign of life of any kind.

'So, this is Refusis,' Dodo exclaimed, some of her apprehension having disappeared. 'Where's the red carpet then?'

Number Nine looked around warily. 'The Refusians must be hiding somewhere. We must find them.' He signalled to the party to start walking. 'Move carefully. And don't forget that I am still armed!'

He held up his weapon to illustrate the point.

The Doctor shrugged and elected to lead the way, taking the party away from the parked Launcher. He noticed, as they moved along, that it was beautiful country that surrounded them. Dales, rivers and tumbling waterfalls . . . and above it all, blue skies with a scattering of white clouds, instead of the steel roof that covered the Ark's surface.

But no sooner had they moved away from the Launcher than something – or someone – entered it. But even had they stayed they would not have seen its entry . . . for it was an invisible being.

Indentations appeared on one of the seats as it sat down. It was obviously curious about the craft and operated the door lever. The door closed . . . and then, as the lever was operated again, re-opened.

The being sighed, obviously pleased with its find. Then it stepped out of the door, disturbing the nearby bushes as it moved away from the Launcher.

Number Nine was puzzled. 'I see no signs of life. Perhaps the findings of the audio space research were wrong. It looks as though there are no such beings as Refusians.'

The Doctor smiled. 'In that case let us return to the Launcher and send a message back to the Ark. We can tell them that they can make their landings quite safely!' He chuckled. 'I am sure they will be extremely delighted to hear it.'

Dodo agreed. 'A good idea, because it will take some time to get the whole of the population down here.'

'Don't worry,' Number Nine replied. 'It may not take as long as you think.'

'What do you mean?' Dodo asked sharply. 'Are you Monoids up to something?'

For a moment Number Nine was uncertain in his reply, caught off-guard. 'Er ... what I mean to say is ... no!'

'No? But you gave yourself away, didn't you?' Dodo persisted. She looked at him appraisingly. 'I've got a feeling that when the time comes you're not going to bring the Guardians down here at all. Is that it?'

The Guardian Yendom interjected nervously. 'But they promised ...'

'I don't care,' said Dodo. 'I'm right, aren't I?'

The Doctor had been wandering about, taking a second and more careful look at their surroundings. Now he called back: 'We were all wrong! This place *is* inhabited.' He beckoned them to him. 'Come! See for yourselves!'

Puzzled, they hurried to his side. Then, following his pointed finger, they saw, in a distance, a building.

'Why ... it's a castle!' Dodo cried.

Number Nine studied it thoughtfully. He voiced his thoughts. 'Why didn't the Refusians see us arrive? ... Or make any moves to stop us?'

'Shall we find out?' the Doctor asked.

Number Nine nodded. 'Proceed!'

With the Doctor leading the way, they set out across the

countryside that separated them from the castle.

It took them some time. On the way the Doctor quietly addressed the Guardian Yendom. 'How long have you served the Monoids?' he asked.

'All my life,' Yendom replied in a low voice. 'My father before me.' He glanced back at Number Nine. 'And now the thought, after all this, that they might desert us ... it doesn't bear thinking about.'

'Perhaps you should have stayed loyal to your kind?' the Doctor suggested.

'But I have!' Yendom replied. 'So have all of us who have served our masters. It was our way of ensuring our future.' He grimaced. 'Oh, I know that the others – the ones who resisted – despise us, but I still think our way has been right.'

'Perhaps,' the Doctor observed. 'But you'll soon learn which of you employed the right tactics, won't you?'

The castle lay before them, surrounded by a moat, but with the bridge down and its large wooden doors open. They entered it, making their way through a court-yard into the hall of the keep. They paused as they looked around.

'It is deserted!' Number Nine said.

The Doctor nodded. 'Very strange indeed!'

He and Dodo started searching in the anterooms that led into the main hall. Number Nine shook his head.

'There is no-one in this place!' he stated.

'How can you be so sure?' the Doctor asked.

'They must be hiding somewhere,' Number Nine concluded. 'That must be because they are just frightened creatures.'

'I don't like this place,' Dodo said. 'It's ... so weird.'

'What do you mean?' the Doctor asked.

'It's just a feeling I've got,' she replied. 'I mean ... this looks like an old castle ... but it's so clean.'

'Why, of course!' the Doctor agreed.

'What does that mean?' Yendom asked.

'The child has noted that there is no dust ... anywhere. If it were totally uninhabited, then the dust would have collected and there would be cobwebs all over the place.'

'Cobwebs?' Yendom asked, puzzled.

'Er ... never mind.' The Doctor looked around. 'But there is more to this place than meets the eye.'

'I would like to see the faces of these Refusians,' Number Nine declared.

'I'm not sure I would,' Dodo remarked. 'If they're anything like you, I've seen enough!'

'What's that?'

'Oh ... nothing.' She muttered to the Doctor, 'Why can't I keep my mouth shut?'

'Something I've often wondered, dear child,' he answered drily.

Number Nine had walked over to a large table and there picked up a china figurine. 'I will challenge them!' he cried out. 'Like this!' He hurled the figurine across the hall so that it smashed into pieces when it hit the wall.

'What are you doing?' Dodo cried out.

The Doctor also protested. 'That is no way to establish friendship ...' he declared.

'They must be brought out into the open,' Number Nine answered. 'They will not be able to hide forever!'

He picked up a vase and raised it threateningly over his head. As he did so, the flower it contained fell out and landed on the floor. But just as Number Nine was about to throw the vase against the wall a voice boomed out: 'Put it down! Your friend is right!'

Startled, Number Nine looked around. But there was no sign of anyone.

'Where did that voice come from?' Number Nine demanded.

'I think ... from up there.' Yendom indicated a broad flight of stairs.

'No!' Dodo said. 'More like this room here ...'

Number Nine looked around, glaring. 'Where are you?' He raised the vase higher. 'Show yourself ... or I will smash this into pieces!'

98

The voice boomed again: 'I warned you! Put that down!'

The Doctor looked round appraisingly. 'I think the voice comes from within this room!' he stated.

'Nonsense!' Number Nine replied. 'If the Refusian seeks to challenge me I will accept it and ...'

'You have been warned!' the voice repeated.

Number Nine drew his arm back, intending to throw the vase. But as he did so he was grappled in a vice-like grip by an unseen being. The Monoid attempted to break free of the hold upon him ... but, after a moment, he was forced to ease the vase back down on the table.

'Thank you!' the voice said.

As Number Nine, the Doctor and the others watched, the fallen flower was picked up from the floor and placed back in the vase.

The voice spoke again: 'As your friend said, I am here ... in the hall ... with you!'

The Doctor chuckled, then went over to Number Nine and gently pushed down the weapon in his hand. 'My dear fellow ... you won't need that any more!'

Number Nine was perplexed. For once he was caught off-guard and did not protest as the weapon was lowered.

In the Main Court Chamber aboard the Ark, Number One addressed Number Two.

'They must have landed by now,' he said. 'So we should be getting a report from Number Nine.'

'Yes, Number One.'

Number One rose from his chair and walked out of the Chamber, followed by Number Two.

'What was the plan you had for getting rid of the Guardians and this spaceship?' Number Two asked.

Number One had led Number Two into the Great Hall.

'A short while after we leave they will disappear in a cloud of dust!' he boasted.

Neither of the Monoids was aware that their conversation

was being overhead by the subservient Guardian, Maharis, as he watched them on a monitor in the Main Comfort Chamber. His hand flew nervously to his mouth when he heard this exchange and he listened intently as the Monoids continued talking.

'You mean ... a bomb of some kind?' Number Two asked.

Number One nodded. 'A fission device. I had it made secretly and it is ready to be detonated at any time.'

'But where is it?'

Number One pointed. In the Main Comfort Chamber Maharis desperately tried to follow the direction of his gesture, but the spot that Number One was indicating was out of the Monitor's range. Frightened, he backed away from the screen, uncertain what to do.

Number Two nodded in satisfied agreement, evidently considering the hiding place chosen for the bomb a good one.

'Excellent, Number One,' he said approvingly.

'The last place the Guardians would think of looking for it,' Number One said. 'Even if they suspected its presence aboard the Ark.'

'Why should they?' Number Two asked with a shrug. 'And when it goes off that will be the end of all human existence!'

In the Security Kitchen Steven worked along with the others, preparing food. He was fascinated when Venussa introduced a microparticle into a container of water and it immediately turned into several kilos of mixed organic vegetables.

'So that's one of the ways in which you have been able to travel for seven hundred years,' he observed. 'Those microdots of food – saves a lot of storage space.'

'Everything had to be organised down to the smallest detail,' she replied. 'Even the water is made from micro-crystals.'

Then she looked toward the door as Maharis entered the kitchen, using his Monoid Security Pass. Steven noticed the way in which she reacted at the sight of Maharis.

'Who's he?' he asked.

'His name is Maharis.'

'But you and the others in here seem to resent him.'

'That's because he's a subservient.' As Steven looked at her blankly, she went on. 'He collaborates with the Monoids.'

Maharis was trying to gain their attention. 'I can tell you something,' he said insistently. 'Something terrible!'

Dassuk glared at him. 'Whatever you have to say, why should we believe it?'

Maharis replied: 'Because what I have to say is true. And it threatens all Guardians – prisoners and subservients alike.'

Dassuk and Venussa exchanged glances.

'That's the first time I've heard him admit his true position,' Venussa remarked.

She and the others gathered around Maharis. 'What is it?' Dassuk asked. 'Not that we have to believe anything you have to say. You speak with the voice of the Monoids.'

'No!' Maharis protested. 'No longer. They plan to betray us all! Even those of us who work for them!'

'Betray?' Steven asked. 'How?'

'They will leave behind a device when they land on Refusis. And that device will destroy the Ark and everything in it!'

'How do you know this?' Venussa asked.

'I overheard Number One telling Number Two.'

'Do you know where the device is?' Dassuk asked.

'No. I only heard them talking. I couldn't see where Number One pointed at the position of the bomb ... But I have to get back, otherwise I will be charged with loitering.'

Maharis scuttled out of the Kitchen.

'He is like the jelly that we sometime make,' remarked Dassuk scornfully.

'Somehow we shall have to find out where that bomb is located,' said Steven. 'The question is, how?'

The Doctor walked in the gardens of the castle, deep in conversation with the unseen Refusian.

While he strolled, Number Nine watched the Doctor from a distance. It disturbed him to think that the Doctor was not just talking to himself, as it appeared, but that he was in conversation with a being more powerful than himself and all other Monoids. As he sat on a stone bench observing the Doctor, he took care never to let his attention wander. And his hand never strayed from the heat gun at his side.

' '... and that was the Guardians' aim,' the Doctor explained, 'along with the Monoids' forebears, who were peaceful beings then – to land here on Refusis and inhabit it.'

'Yes, we've known the plan for some time,' the Refusian confirmed. 'And we welcomed it. That's why we built places like this. Together with whole cities, ready for occupation.'

'I see,' the Doctor nodded, impressed. 'Just to make them comfortable.' Shrewdly he added: 'I didn't think you needed places like this for yourselves.'

The Refusian chuckled. 'No! Once we had a shape and form something like you. Then there was a galactic accident – a giant solar flare – and now we no longer have a physical presence that you can see or recognise.'

'But ... er ... can you see each other?'

'Not even that. Oh, we can sense one another, but that is all ... One moment.'

Flowers were disturbed alongside the path. The Doctor watched, fascinated, and realised that the unseen being was plucking weeds from around them. Then, as the being moved on, the Doctor was able to locate his presence by the position of the weeds which he still carried. So now the Doctor appeared to be accompanying a bunch of weeds that hovered and floated along in the air!

'And since we can only sense one another,' the Refusian continued, 'it would have been good for our planet to be once again inhabited by life – visible life, that is – provided that the beings who come here are peaceful.'

Number Nine, watching from a distance, had seen the weeds plucked and saw them travelling through the air near the Doctor. He realised what this meant and reached out for his heat gun and levelled it up.

Out of the corner of his eye the Doctor had caught this movement. Quickly he reached out and snatched the weeds away.

'I'll carry these for you,' he said. 'And I think you had better walk on my other side.'

Number Nine fired his heat gun at the area where the weeds had been, then reacted in annoyance when the blast travelled on past the Doctor and hit a far wall, shattering it to pieces.

The Refusian, now on the other side of the Doctor, spoke: 'I take your point, Doctor. And thank you.'

'My pleasure,' the Doctor replied.

'That Monoid is not a peaceful thing! Sooner or later I think I will have to teach him a firm lesson.'

Number One tried to make contact with Number Nine on the planet. 'This is the Ark calling. Make your report, Number Nine. We need it if we are to know how to act.'

There was no reply. After a moment Number One turned to Number Two. 'He must be making a survey,' he suggested.

'Yes, Number One.'

'If the circumstances are favourable, we land. But if they are not, then we must think in terms of an alternative destination.'

'Where might that be, Number One?'

'That is the problem. There is another planet – Trang – but it will take a long time for the Ark to reach it. You and I would no longer be young by the time we arrived.'

'If that happens and we have to take the second choice, what about the fission bomb? Can it be dismantled to ensure our safe journey?'

'Yes. The timing device would be removed – then it would be safe.'

'You think of everything, Number One. That is why you are a great leader.'

Number One nodded. He recalled that his leadership went back through several generations of his Monoid family – back to the time of the revolution which had enabled the Monoids to wrest control of the Ark from the Guardians.

In that period, when the war had been fought, his forebear had emerged from the ranks of the Monoids. There had been a struggle for the position of leader, but that grand old Monoid had seen off all opposition and had then united the Monoids against the real enemy, the Guardians.

Some Monoids had wanted that war to end in both senses; to win the battle and then to strike up an alliance with some of the Guardians. But Monoid One the First had been quick to denounce this as treachery, and those who had proposed the plan had been condemned and executed. And that had been the right action at the time. Any weakening of resolve at that point and the Guardians might have been able to insinuate their way back into power.

Instead, the Monoids ruled firmly. The Monoid Order answered to no-one except itself and he, Number One the Seventeenth, was the one who organised their every move. And the stewardship of the Guardians, subservients and prisoners alike.

He was proud of his family line, proud of himself and the way he carried out his tasks. It pleased him to think that when they settled on a new planet he would be the one they would refer to in the annals of history as the founder of the new civilisation.

Once again he tried to make contact with Refusis: 'Number Nine ... this is Number One, calling from the Ark.'

There was still no reply. He addressed Number Two: 'I am very curious about what is happening on the planet Refusis ... and what Number Nine and the others have found ...'

Dodo had been wandering through the castle, delighting in its furnishings and the well-stocked closets of clothes that had thoughtfully been put there.

But then she jumped as a female voice addressed her: 'Hello!'

Dodo looked around, but could see no-one; and then realised that this was a female of the Refusian species.

'Hi!' she replied. 'Made me jump out of my skin. I don't think I'll get used to something – I mean, someone – that I can't even see.'

'We'll have to think up a way of putting your mind at rest on that point,' laughed the Refusian girl, in a reassuring tone.

'Well, for starters, do you have a name? . . . Mine's Dodo.'

'Normally we haven't, but that's no reason why we shouldn't start using them. Let's see . . . I'll call myself Mary . . . and my brother – that's the Refusian you've already met – we'll call him . . . Charles.'

'Mary and Charles. Yeah, OK. That sounds fine.'

'Do you like this place that we've prepared for you?'

'Yes! Reminds me of a castle in Wales. Castle Coch, it's called. That means – in Welsh – the Red Castle.'

'And the clothes you were looking at?'

'Great! Fab gear!'

'Fab gear? Is that Welsh, too?'

'Oh, no! Just my way of coming across. But please don't tell the Doctor. He's always having a go at me about the way I speak.'

The Refusian girl laughed. 'I won't tell him.' Then she moved to a door, as Dodo realised when she saw it opening. 'Come with me. I'll show you something.'

Puzzled, Dodo followed the voice, which chatted on in a friendly way, describing the various things they passed, until eventually they emerged outside, onto a tennis court.

'Do you play this game?' the Refusian girl asked.

'Well, I have knocked a ball around a bit in my time,' Dodo replied cautiously. In fact, this was a considerable under-statement. She had played tennis at school and had gone on to win a county championship.

'I've been dying for a game,' came the eager reply. 'So you play from this end and I'll go to the other.'

A tennis racket, seemingly of its own accord, jumped into Dodo's hands. She caught it, then watched as another racket was borne through the air to the far end of the court.

'Ready?' her opponent called out.

'Er ... yes.'

Above the racket opposite her a ball was lobbed into the air. Then, as it descended, it was struck with tremendous force so that it came flying over the net and aced Dodo. She stared in amazement. The ball had travelled too fast for her even to attempt a return.

'Er ... sorry ... I wasn't as ready as I thought I was,' she said lamely.

Then she picked up the ball and played it down the court. Only to be distracted once more as she saw the racket at the far end moving across the base line to cover it. The racket swung ... and again the ball went past Dodo like a cannon shot.

They played on for a while and Dodo managed to recover some of her skill as she learned to accept the bobbing, darting racket for what it was – the only opponent that she could see.

At the same time she was somewhat relieved when the Doctor opened a window and called out: 'Dodo ... come up here.'

'Have to go,' she called out to her opponent. 'We could have another game another time.'

'I'll look forward to that,' came the answer. 'I've enjoyed our game, Dodo.'

'Yeah!' Dodo put her racket down and started back indoors. 'Be seeing you – in a manner of speaking, that is!'

In the Great Hall Number Four looked up at the statue that towered over him and Number Seven.

'The body of a humanoid ... the head of a Monoid,' Number Four murmured. 'Maybe that was the way it was meant to be – a fusion of our two beings.'

'Careful!' Number Seven answered. 'If any of the others heard and reported your thoughts back to Number One it could mean trouble for you.'

Number Four nodded, accepting the point. But at the same time he was troubled. He cared for the future of his fellow creatures, the Monoids. But he was uneasy about where the leadership of Number One was taking them. He had often questioned decisions, but carefully, going only so far and never allowing any hint of protest to go over the brink into outright confrontation.

His forebears had often adopted the same attitude. That streak in their family had long been recognised by Number One and his forebears, but had always been tolerated as long as it had not gone too far.

Now he questioned in his mind the total enslavement of the Guardians, whether by their use as volunteer servants or as slave labour. It had always seemed to Number Four that this was a mismanagement of the talents that they could genuinely offer; after all, long ago their forefathers had achieved a high level of civilisation on Earth. They had evaluated and correctly predicted the eventual fate of that same Earth and had taken the right decision to leave it, and they had designed and built the spaceship that they were all now travelling in.

Humanoids and Monoids, together then, working as a team. Oh, yes ... the Monoids had been taken for granted; their willing co-operation had led to their being exploited as mere labour. But Number Four had a feeling that many of the Guardians now recognised that as a mistake, while at the same time they were undeniably having to suffer a worse fate than the Monoids had ever endured.

And then there was the bomb that would destroy the Guardians, hidden somewhere on the Ark by that cunning Number One. He glanced over to where a party of humanoids were being ushered through the hall by another armed Monoid and, for a moment, felt sorry for them.

Number Four was not happy. He would have to keep close observation on developments in the future, even if that meant more questions for Number One. In the meantime, he wondered about the party that was making the survey of

Refusis at that very moment.

When Dodo arrived back in the hall, Number Nine was addressing the Doctor and the Guardian Yendom.

'We must return to the Launcher. We must warn Number One and the others so that we can deal with these unseen creatures, the Refusians.'

The Doctor glanced at a chair where he knew the Refusian was seated. But the being chose not to speak. Instead, Yendom stepped forward and addressed Number Nine.

'We? Meaning only the Monoids?' With rising apprehension he went on. 'When you spoke of it before you meant that only you and your kind would make the landings, didn't you?'

Number Nine started out of the hall.

'Yendom, I do not have to account to you!' He pointed his weapon at the Guardian. 'Now, come with me, and let us pass on our vital information.'

Yendom followed Number Nine out of the hall.

Dodo watched them go. 'I don't think Number Nine is too happy.' She moved to the chair to sit down. 'Nor is that Guardian ...'

Before she could sit the Doctor grabbed her arm.

'Not there, my dear. That seat is taken.'

'Eh?' Dodo gaped. Then she jumped back as the Refusian spoke.

'You two stay here,' he said.

'OK ... Charlie!'

'Charlie?' echoed the Doctor, with a puzzled frown. 'What's this, my dear?'

'Oh ... I've met his sister. And she wants to be called Mary, and we agreed that Charlie – Charles – was a nice name for him.'

'I am delighted with that thought,' the voice replied. 'But now I will see what the Monoid is up to.'

The Doctor and Dodo watched as the door of the hall

swung closed.

Some distance from the castle Yendom grasped Number Nine's arm.

'I ... I will not let you contact the other Monoids!'

Number Nine pushed him back. 'Yendom, stay away from me. Keep your distance.'

'No! If you alert them they will start landing here, then destroy the Ark and everyone aboard!'

He closed in on Number Nine again. But this time the reptilian Monoid raised its heat gun and directed it at Yendom. There was a flash ... and where Yendom had stood, only scorched earth remained.

From within the castle the Doctor had seen the flash of the heat gun. Worried, he turned to Dodo.

'I don't think we should stay here, doing nothing,' he said. 'That Number Nine may have found a way of attacking ... Charles.'

'Oh, I wouldn't think so, Doctor. The Refusians are very strong.'

'What makes you say that?'

'Well, I played a game of tennis with Mary ...'

'*Tennis!*'

'Yes. And judging by some of her shots and the force behind them, she – and I think any of them – could wipe the floor with the competition at Wimbledon and every other tournament with no trouble at all!'

The Doctor sighed. 'Nevertheless, let's see what we can find out.'

Number Nine had entered the Launcher, laying the heat gun down on the seat near him. He spoke into the relay system.

'Refusis Launcher to the spaceship Ark.'

The reply came immediately from Number One. 'Yes, Number Nine! Give us your report. Are the landings possible?'

'The planet offers everything we need. But I must warn you ...'

'Yes?' Number One interrupted impatiently.

'Listen to this carefully. When we first arrived we ...'

He did not notice as he spoke that just outside the open door the shrubbery was being disturbed. The Refusian moved close to the Launcher.

'... encountered some very strange –' Number Nine continued. But then he broke off as the Launcher suddenly tilted crazily. Amazed, Number Nine glanced out to see that it was being raised high into the air ... was being whirled around in a way that made him giddy as he desperately tried to hang on. Then it was flung away by some mighty, invisible force.

As the Launcher crashed to the ground a gigantic explosion ripped it apart, scattering debris over the landscape.

The Refusian had indeed taught Number Nine a lesson.

As they hurried toward the Launcher the Doctor and Dodo heard the explosion. Puzzled and alarmed, they ran through the woodlands until they found the spot where the Launcher had been resting.

It was now totally destroyed, its shattered remnants strewn all about. Dodo looked at the wreckage in dismay.

'What do we do now?' she asked.

'Nothing, my dear. We shall have to wait until the next party from the Ark lands!'

'But what if they don't come? What if they decide to find another planet?'

The Doctor shrugged resignedly.

'In that case, my dear, we'll just have to stay here!'

7

Search

In the Control Room aboard the Ark, Number One spoke urgently into the relay link:

'Number Nine! Number Nine ... give us your report.'

No answer. Number One impatiently abandoned his attempts to make contact with Refusis.

'Why doesn't Number Nine give us his report?' Number Two asked.

'I don't know. It could be a simple break in communications ... or it could be something else.'

'Something else? What?'

'It could be that he was attacked!'

'But the report he started seemed to suggest that conditions on the planet Refusis were favourable.'

'Yes.'

'Then what can we do, Number One?'

Number One paced away from the control modules, deep in thought. There were several possible courses of action open to him ... but then he made up his mind and firmly turned to address Number Two and other Monoids who were gathered in the Control Room.

'We will proceed,' he stated. 'We will prepare ourselves for the main landings.'

Number Two nodded in agreement. He addressed the others: 'Number One has spoken! Make the launchers ready for the landings and get the Monoid population trays prepared for the journey!'

Number One had already left the Control Room and was now followed by Number Two. Others also followed, to carry out their allotted tasks.

But Number Four hung back, addressing Number Seven. 'The Leader has spoken. He has said that we must go. But supposing that he is wrong? We are still not certain what Refusis is like.'

Number Seven nodded thoughtfully.

The Doctor and Dodo had left the spot where the Launcher lay in ruins and were making their way back to the castle.

'Marooned on a strange planet,' Dodo moaned. 'Millions of miles from nowhere . . . and millions of years from the time when I was born!'

'Oh, come on, my child.'

She paused, suddenly horrified by a thought. 'That means I must be at least . . . *ten million years old*!'

The Doctor looked at her quizzically. 'Now you mustn't worry about little things like that. You're looking very well on it.'

'All right for you to say that! Heaven knows how long you've been around.'

'A fair old time, I grant you.'

'So you're used to the idea. But I'm not.' She sighed. 'What I wouldn't give to be back in my own time and . . .'

'Well, what would you be doing at this moment?'

'I'd be out shopping . . . new clothes . . . and planning on going to a disco!'

The Doctor looked around at the green fields and forests that surrounded them. 'I always knew that there was something to be said for this place. Now I know what it is.'

'What?'

'Peace!'

Dodo snorted: 'Too much of that and life can get to be dead boring.'

They both turned, startled, when a female voice spoke to them from out of nowhere. 'Hello, Dodo.'

The Doctor stared at the direction from which the voice had come. 'Who's that?' he asked.

'This is Mary,' answered Dodo. 'You remember; I told you about her. The tennis player . . . Charlie's sister.'

112

'Oh, yes, of course,' the Doctor acknowledged. He bowed slightly in the direction of the voice. 'How do you do, my dear?'

'I am very well,' the voice replied. 'And you sound in fine form, Doctor.'

'Ah! So you've heard of me?'

'My brother has told me about you.' There was a rustle of leaves in bushes as she moved closer. 'But you don't sound very happy, Dodo?'

'Well, it's a nice place ...' Dodo said.

'But I gather you would not like to stay here forever?'

'Don't take it personally,' Dodo said quickly. 'But back where I come from I've got all me own mates and ...'

'I understand perfectly,' the voice replied. 'Travel broadens the mind ... but there's no place like home, is there?'

'That's it!'

'Then perhaps one day ... but, meanwhile, my brother is waiting for you. *Au revoir!*'

There was a rustle among the foliage and they realised that the Refusian girl had left them.

'I told you she was nice,' said Dodo.

'Yes. But now let's go to the castle.'

Number One studied a large galactic hologram in the Main Hall. He indicated Refusis to Number Two.

'At last!' he breathed triumphantly. 'A new planet of our own! Where we can establish our own way of life!'

Number Two nodded. But then he noticed Number Four conferring with Number Seven on the far side of the hall. Employing the lip-reading art of old, Number Two was able to make out what the other Monoid was saying.

'Number One was right to send out a forward party,' Number Four said. 'But I have the feeling that he is not right to proceed when the report from that mission was so incomplete.'

'It is a rash thing to do,' Number Seven agreed.

Number Two plucked at Number One's sleeve. 'Number One ... a word of warning.'

'What's that?'

'Number Four is beginning to question the wisdom of your leadership. Even at this moment he is conferring with Number Seven in secrecy.'

Number One chuckled complacently.

'Don't worry about that,' he replied in a confident tone. 'At the slightest sign of opposition we can easily get rid of them. As easily as we will destroy this ship once we have left it. Remember the final answer – the fission bomb!'

The voice of the Refusian greeted the Doctor and Dodo as they entered the main hall of the castle.

'We are, as you must realise, concerned about the arrival of the Ark,' the voice stated, 'and what it will mean to this planet.'

'Yes,' the Doctor replied, 'I can quite understand that. That, I take it, is why you destroyed the Launcher?'

'Yes. I was loath to take that action because here we have always known peace, never war or conflict.'

'You're not the only ones like that, Charlie,' Dodo interjected. 'You know, the Guardians – the human beings who travel in the Ark – they used to have your ideas, too!'

'Yes, that's true!' the Doctor agreed. 'But on the other hand you mustn't think they were perfect.'

'What do you mean?' Dodo asked.

'Sometimes they were extremely intolerant and selfish.'

'Is that why they were conquered by the Monoids?' the Refusian asked.

'Exactly!' the Doctor answered.

'Maybe so,' Dodo cut in. 'But there are some among the Guardians who wouldn't mind having a go at rising up against the Monoids and trying to do better!'

'Then we will allow them time to make their attempt,' the

114

Refusian decided. 'We will allow the passing of one day before we think in terms of employing defensive measures.'

'Yes,' the Doctor agreed. 'One day! Thank you!'

Dodo spoke to the Doctor. 'Now it's up to Steven and the others.'

'Quite so, my dear,' the Doctor said. 'Quite so. And there's nothing that we can do at this moment to help them!'

In the Security Kitchen aboard the Ark Steven had been peering out through a porthole.

'The Monoids are up to something,' he told the others in the kitchen. 'They're rushing about all over the place.'

'Do you think they're preparing to leave the Ark?' Venussa asked.

'Probably!' he replied. He looked around desperately. 'Isn't there any way we can get out of this kitchen?'

'None,' she replied. 'The walls are thick and the doors can only be opened from the outside.'

'Who opens them?'

'*They* do!' Dassuk replied. 'Sometimes the subservient Guardians ... Maharis, for instance.'

'Then we must get him to help us.'

'He won't. He's too frightened!'

Steven considered this as he paced restlessly. Then he announced: 'All right! In that case we'll have to get his help without his knowing it!'

Maharis walked through a corridor carrying a tray loaded with refreshments. On his way he passed a group of prisoner Guardians who were being escorted by an armed Monoid. The prisoners glared at him with contempt and loathing. He hurried on, trying to avoid their hostile stares, until he met and greeted another subservient Guardian.

'What's going on?' the other Guardian asked. 'All this activity ...'

'It's only to be expected, now that the Ark is close to Refusis,' Maharis replied.

Maharis was suddenly cautious. He had already spoken in haste to the prisoners in the kitchen and now regretted it. Because even if the Monoids were intent on destroying the Guardians, there was the chance that some might be spared, if only to serve. And if there was that chance then he wanted to be one of the favoured ones and there was no point in spreading alarm to others, for any reaction on their part might doom him.

'I'll be glad to be out of this spaceship and on that planet,' the Guardian said.

'Er ... yes.'

The Guardian studied Maharis enviously. 'I suppose you will be one of the first to be taken there,' he remarked. 'After all, you are the honoured servant of Number One.'

'I suppose that could be true.'

'Whereas I ... I am the servant to Number Thirty-Five. Why, he is not even a member of the Grand Council! So I suppose I will be a long way down the list of those who'll land.'

'It is only a matter of patience,' Maharis ventured, placatingly.

'You have always been lucky, Maharis! Your father, and generations before you, served the masters.' He sighed. 'I wish my forebears had had the sense to do the same thing.'

'Yes ... but now you must excuse me. Number One is expecting this.' He indicated the food on the tray.

He walked on, leaving the other Guardian staring after him in envy.

In the Launch Bay area Number Five was supervising the loading of a craft.

Guardians loaded sealed containers in stacks aboard the Launcher. Number Five watched them carefully and called out: 'Be careful! Remember, each container has twenty trays

... and each tray contains a thousand Monoids!'

His heat weapon was in his hands as he watched over them. 'They were thoughtfully preserved in microcell form by your ancestors. They must reach their new life on Refusis safely!'

The Guardians went on working, obeying his bidding.

Maharis had delivered the tray of food to Number One in the Main Comfort Chamber. Number Two was speaking to his leader.

'Everything is proceeding according to plan, Number One. We must have –'

Number One stayed him for a moment while he turned to address Maharis. 'Thank you, Maharis. That will be all.'

Maharis, who had hoped to hover and hear more, nodded, bowed and withdrew.

Number One watched him go and there was contempt in his voice when he said: 'Stupid, trusting creature! He and all his kind are still under the illusion that they will be coming with us to Refusis.'

'They deserve their fate!' said Number Two scornfully.

'Yes!' Number One leaned forward. 'What were you going to say?'

'I was reporting that the loading of the Launchers was proceeding satisfactorily.'

'Good! Then you and I and all the other Monoids will leave shortly!'

The Doctor was thoughtful.

'If only there were some way we could help Steven and the others,' he mused. 'But there's nothing we can do. Now that the Launcher is destroyed we can't even establish elementary contact with them.'

'I know how you feel,' Dodo said. 'I feel the same way ... helpless!'

The Refusian addressed them. 'There is no sense in

worrying about things that you cannot influence for the moment. Try and relax. For instance . . .' a drawer in the table was opened '. . . we could play a game of chess.'

The Refusian brought the game out and placed it on the table. Dodo stared at it, uncertainly.

'Well, that game is not exactly my bag, Charlie,' she said. 'But you two go ahead and play.'

As the Doctor and the Refusian set the pieces out, the latter moving them with unseen hands, the Refusian chuckled. 'I am beginning to like my name. "Charlie!" Tell me, is it a popular name?'

'Oh, yes!' Dodo replied. 'There was Charlie the First and Charlie the Second and –'

'Charlie Chaplin!' the Doctor interjected. 'Yes, we know, my dear! Now why don't you run along and find something else to amuse you, h'm?'

Mary suddenly spoke out.

'Come with me, Dodo. We can have another look at those dresses upstairs.'

'OK,' Dodo replied, bouncing up. 'I don't know how you feel, Mary, but I sometimes find certain men a bit dull!'

She started up the stairs, knowing that the Refusian girl was at her side. The Doctor sighed, then glanced at the board. He addressed the chair opposite him.

'Yours is the first move, my dear sir.'

'Thank you.'

The Refusian moved a piece forward, and the two of them settled down to enjoy the game.

At the head of the stairs Dodo paused and addressed her unseen companion.

'Mind you . . . men being dull . . . that doesn't include Steven! He's OK . . . and I'll bet he's having a go at something right now!'

Steven, aided by Venussa, was plumping out a bed in the rest area in the Security Kitchen.

He was attempting to create an illusion of the bed being occupied. It took several moments of plopping the blankets and pillows. Then he and Venussa stepped back, satisfied.

When Maharis entered the kitchen, Baccu was strained against the door frame. Maharis didn't notice as he brought an empty tray forward and placed it on the table. He turned to go out but Venussa delayed him.

'Maharis!'

As he turned to look at her questioningly, his back to the door, Baccu quietly slipped out of the kitchen.

'Yes?' Maharis asked.

'What's the news from outside?'

'The Monoids are preparing to leave,' he replied, nervously.

'And are you hoping that they will take you?' Dassuk asked.

'Why not?' Maharis said. 'We can serve the Monoids just as well on Refusis as we have done here.' Then he glanced around. 'Just a moment! Where's Baccu?'

'Asleep,' said Venussa. She indicated the bed that Steven and she had made up. Maharis looked at the bed. Satisfied, he turned and made his way out of the kitchen.

Outside, Baccu was hidden behind a column. He watched as Maharis left the area, then looked around to make sure that he was not being observed. Stealthily he returned to the Security Kitchen door and pressed a palm-panel. The door slid open and Steven, Venussa, Dassuk and the others joined him outside.

'Hurry!' Steven urged. 'We had better split into twos and start searching for that bomb as fast as we can go!'

They murmured assent and went off in different directions, fanning out through the spaceship.

'I am not even sure I'll know what a bomb looks like,' said Venussa anxiously as she accompanied Steven.

'Just let me know if you see anything unusual,' he replied. 'All I know is that we haven't got much time!'

*

Number One was striding through the Great Hall when Number Two hurried to join him. He quickly spoke to his leader.

'There has still been no further contact from Number Nine on Refusis, Number One.'

'Never mind that! Give the signal for the mass landings to begin at once!'

Number Two repeated the order into his wrist communicator. This order was taken up in the Control Room and a Monoid pressed hard on a large button.

Immediately, throughout the Ark, the echo of a klaxon was heard, blaring forth, and in the Launching Bays teams of technicians prepared craft for expulsion.

Numbers Four and Seven boarded a Launcher in the bay.

Number Four spoke: 'The moment we land we will decide whether Number One is to stay as our Leader. If Refusis is dangerous, then we must return to the Ark before it is destroyed!'

Number Seven nodded in agreement. Then the door of the Launcher was closed behind them, and they felt the power surge as it was propelled away from the spaceship.

As they hurried down a corridor, Steven and Venussa were brought to a halt by the echoing signal.

'What's that?' asked Steven.

'The mass landing order,' she replied.

'So they aren't going to wait any longer . . . and meanwhile our time is running out!'

They both sped on, hastily checking each room for possible hiding places.

Numbers One and Two were in their Launcher, ready for the thrust that would send them out on the last stage of their journey.

'What about the bomb?' Number Two asked.

'It is ready! It is timed to go off twelve hours from now!'

They tensed as their Launcher was thrust out into space, joining and becoming part of a fleet of such craft that were leaving the mother ship and heading in the direction of Refusis, leaving Maharis and the other subservient Guardians in their wake, crowding into the now empty Launching Bays.

'They've gone!' Maharis cried out desperately. 'And they have left us behind!'

In the castle on Refusis the Doctor and the Refusian were locked in battle on the final moves of their chess game. Dodo came back down the stairs and glanced over the Doctor's shoulder.

'That knight,' she whispered. 'Move it forward.'

The Doctor considered, calculating the outcome, then followed her suggestion.

Immediately the Refusian moved another piece and took the knight, while at the same time exclaiming: 'Checkmate!'

The Doctor puffed out his cheeks in annoyance. But there was nothing he could do about it. He shrugged as he conceded.

'Foolish girl!' he chided. 'I was holding my own until you made that suggestion ...'

'Yes! But I wasn't on your side,' said Dodo. 'I was on Charlie's!'

The Refusian girl called from the window: 'Something seems to be going on! There are some more craft landing on our planet.'

Hastily the others joined her at the window, staring out. The Launchers could be seen landing a short distance away. The Doctor snorted and remarked: 'That must be the main party of the Monoids.'

*

Steven and Venussa turned a corner and met Dassuk and another Guardian.

'Any luck?' Steven asked. 'Any sight of the bomb?'

'No.'

'We haven't found anything, either.' Then they looked up as Maharis approached them.

He was distraught. 'They have gone . . . and they've left us behind, despite all their promises.'

'You were wrong to trust them in the first place!' said Venussa coldly.

'But just a minute,' Steven cut in. 'You were close to them, Maharis. Isn't there anything that they said that would give us a clue to where the bomb is?'

'No!' Maharis shook his head in desperation. 'I've told you all I know . . . but I never heard any of them speak about it afterwards.'

'Too bad! We could have done with some luck just now.' Steven indicated a corridor. 'But in the meantime round up some of your friends and search places like that.'

Maharis shook his head hopelessly. 'What's the use? There's no sense in trying. The Monoids would have been very clever about the way they concealed it.'

'Don't give in!' Steven snapped. 'Whatever happens, we've got to do everything we can to find that bomb . . . and a way off the Ark!'

He and the others moved on, still swiftly searching, leaving a desolate Maharis in their wake.

The Launchers from the Ark landed in a pattern in the fields and valleys of Refusis. The door levers were operated and the Monoids emerged from the craft to look about them at the planet.

Among the first of this main party were Numbers One and Two. Number One, surveying the landscape curiously, announced: 'Everything seems to be quiet.' He raised the weapon in his hands. 'And from this moment on, this planet is ours!'

'Yes, Number One. This is indeed a proud moment for our kind!' Then Number Two noticed something a short distance away. He walked over to examine it and called out: 'Number One ... look at what I have found.'

Number One went over to join him, and they both stared down at the wreckage of the first Launcher that had landed on Refusis.

'That is the reason why Number Nine failed to complete his message to us!'

'A reason ... and a warning!' Number One said, sombrely. 'We must find out who destroyed this Launcher ... and then destroy them!'

He marched forward, indicating with a wave of his weapon for Number Two and the other Monoids to follow him.

But as they moved away they failed to notice the Doctor and Dodo who were hidden in the undergrowth nearby, watching their every move. When the first group had passed, Dodo made as though to speak, but the Doctor hastily placed his fingers on his lips, urging her to keep silent.

A second group of Monoids came into view. They were headed by Number Four and Number Seven. This group paused uncertainly upon seeing the wreckage of the first Launcher, and Number Four addressed them.

'Number One has made a mistake in bringing us here!' he stated. 'We will have to wait for our chance and then challenge him ... and then return to the Ark. There is still time to find that fission bomb that has been left behind and deal with it before it is too late.'

'I think you are right, Number Four,' Number Seven agreed. He looked at the others. 'Do you agree?'

There was a murmur of assent from them.

'Then come,' Number Four commanded. 'We must not let Number One and the others get out of our sight.'

The group moved on. The Doctor pursed his lips.

'A fission bomb!' he whispered.

'When that other Monoid – Number Nine – hinted that

they had a plan for dealing with the Guardians, I had no idea that it was going to be anything like that!' Dodo said.

'Nor did I, Dodo. But a fission bomb – left like that aboard the Ark – would have a timing device. I just hope that Steven and the others are aware of it and can find it before that device reaches zero!' Seeing that the way was clear he rose to his feet.

'Where are you going?' Dodo asked.

'To one of the Launchers, my child. It's our only chance of warning the Ark!' He started away. 'Come on!'

Dodo followed him.

Steven and Venussa again met up with Dassuk and others as they entered the Control Room together. Steven paused hopelessly, punching the keys that controlled a bank of monitors.

'It could be anywhere,' he said gloomily. 'In the corridors ... in the jungle over there ... in the cultivated lands, the desert ... anywhere!'

'We'll find it,' Venussa said. 'We must!'

Suddenly, as Steven operated the keys controlling the signals, a strange noise echoed forth.

'What's that?' Dassuk asked.

'I'm not sure ...' Steven juggled with the control key, improving the signal that had started coming in. Suddenly it was in line, and they heard the Doctor addressing them: 'Refusis calling! Refusis calling the spaceship Ark.'

Steven spoke quickly into the relay system. 'This is the Ark – and this is Steven speaking, Doctor.'

'Ah, thank heavens, Steven,' the Doctor replied. 'At least you're still alive.' Then he continued urgently. 'Now listen – the Ark is about to be blown up!'

'We know that,' Steven answered. 'But have you any idea where the bomb is hidden?'

'No! But I am going to find out from the Monoids. In the meantime I'll send back some of the Launchers to the Ark. And you must keep searching for that bomb!'

There was a click, and Steven realised that contact had been broken. He turned and addressed the others: 'All right ... you heard what he said ... so let's intensify our search!'

They nodded and scattered to follow his bidding.

In the Launcher, Dodo looked at the Doctor quizzically. 'But how are you going to talk to the Monoids? And how are you going to send the Launchers back to the Ark?'

The voice of the Refusian echoed the quesiton: 'Yes, Doctor ... how?'

The Doctor glanced around in appreciation. 'Oh, I am glad you heard that,' he said. 'You know, these Launchers are simple to operate ... and I would like to suggest that *you* fly this back to the spaceship?'

'Me?'

'Yes! The Monoids won't know who is taking it! And as for me talking to them ... well, that problem is quite simple!'

The Doctor paused expectantly, waiting for a reply.

It came: 'Very well! I will do as you suggest!'

'Ah, thank you, my dear fellow.'

'Yeah! Ta, Charlie!' Dodo added.

The Doctor plucked her sleeve and rose from his seat. They stepped out of the Launcher and started to walk across a field when they were intercepted by a party of Monoids.

'Ah, dear friends!' the Doctor cried. 'So we meet again!'

'Now you've gone and done it!' Dodo whispered.

'Haven't I just?' the Doctor whispered back quickly. 'I said that I would talk to them and in order to do that I must face them ... and one way of achieving that is by being taken prisoner. *Et voilà!*' He spoke up as he addressed the nearest Monoid. 'Welcome to Refusis!'

The Monoid raised his weapon threateningly, pointing it at the Doctor. But Number Twenty-Three called out: 'Don't harm them! ... At least, not yet. Number One will want to question them.' He addressed the Doctor and Dodo. 'You will come with us.'

'Delighted!' the Doctor agreed.

But as they started to walk away, the power source of the Launcher started up and it rose into the air. Number Twenty-Three stared at it, then addressed the Doctor. 'Who is it that travels in that Launcher?' he asked. 'We have seen no-one except yourselves since we have been here.'

'Well, to tell the truth . . .' the Doctor answered, '. . . neither have we!'

Steven entered the Main Comfort Chamber to find Maharis sitting there disconsolately.

'Have you found anything here?' Steven asked.

'What's the use?' Maharis replied. 'There wouldn't be anything in here . . .'

'There is no point in moping and giving in just because the Monoids promised you something and then failed you!' Steven snapped. 'You've got to do something to try and save yourself.'

'I believed in them!' Maharis cried in despair. 'But they betrayed me!'

Dassuk hurried into the chamber. 'Steven, come with me!'

'Why? What has happened?'

'One of the Launchers has returned from Refusis.'

Dassuk led them out of the chamber and to the Launch Bay area. He indicated: 'There! See for yourself!'

The Launcher was at rest on its platform and was now surrounded by Guardians. Its door was open and they were staring in . . . at nothing!

'It was like that when the door opened!' said Venussa. 'Empty!'

But as she, Steven and the others puzzled over this, they were taken aback when the unseen Refusian suddenly laughed!

'May I come aboard?' he asked.

Steven was cautious. 'Who . . . what . . . are you?'

'I am a Refusian,' came the reply. 'And I am a friend of the

Doctor and Dodo.'

They all immediately relaxed, though still not understanding why they couldn't see the Refusian, and Steven answered: 'Why, of course! And welcome to the Ark!'

In the main hall of the castle on Refusis, Number One studied the Doctor with his swivelling eye.

'Doctor ... where are the Refusians?'

'I don't know! I haven't seen one!' the Doctor replied.

'I have a report that says that you stepped out of the Launcher and a moment later it was flown away!' Number One stated. 'It must have been controlled by someone ... and I must find the answer!'

Impatiently, he paced away from the Doctor and Dodo.

'Do you think they will talk, Number One?' Number Two asked him.

'If they don't, they will die!'

His pacing had taken him near Number Four, who spoke up: 'Perhaps! But it would seem that we will die as well.'

'Do you seek to challenge me?' Number One demanded.

'You have led us to this planet and placed us all in danger.'

'If that is the way you feel you can return to the Ark.'

'We will!' Number Four replied, taking up the challenge. 'Only there we have to face another danger that you have created – the fission device.'

'Yes, and that will be quite a problem, I can assure you – finding it and getting rid of it!'

Number Four faced the other Monoids: 'Those of you who wish to stay on this unknown world with its hidden dangers must side with Number One. But those who truly care for the future of the Monoids must come with me!'

There was a moment of uncertainty among them. Then several moved to Number Four's side, while others remained with Number One.

Number Four looked at his supporters, then, with a wave of his weapon, led them out of the castle. Number Two addressed Number One.

'Will you let them go?'

'Why not?' Number One chuckled and turned back to the Doctor and Dodo. 'You see, Doctor, I let traitors choose their own fate. They will be lucky if they find the bomb ... and even if they do, they will not find it easy to dispose of.'

'Why not?' the Doctor asked.

'Oh, come on ... tell us!' Dodo urged. 'After all, we're not going anywhere!'

'The child is right,' the Doctor said. 'So where have you hidden the fission bomb?'

Number One chuckled. 'In the last place they will think of looking,' he gloated. 'It is in the Monoid statue in the Great Hall!'

8

The Final Conflict

In the Control Room Steven addressed Venussa, Dassuk and the others: 'I think we should split up. Some of us should land on Refusis to help the Doctor and Dodo, while the rest of us stay here and try to deal with that bomb.'

'Yes, that's a good idea,' Dassuk agreed.

'Is it?' Maharis protested. 'Why should any of us stay and risk being blown up?'

'Because the Earth's population – and every other form of life – all these things have to be taken to Refusis later!'

'Steven is right,' Venussa said. 'That's why our forefathers started this voyage through space in the first place, seven hundred years ago.'

'But we're alive!' Maharis protested. 'Why should any of us die for an idea that they thought of?'

'You've served too long with the Monoids, Maharis,' said Venussa. 'You no longer belong with us.' She turned to Steven. 'Let him go with the landing party.'

Steven nodded. 'All right.' He turned to Dassuk. 'You take the Launcher – go with him, Maharis – and you two –' he indicated a couple of young Guardians, 'contact the Doctor as soon as you can!'

Another Guardian spoke up: 'I'll stay here.'

'All right.' Steven turned to Venussa. 'What about you?'

'I'll stay, too.'

Those who had been selected to make the trip to Refusis started out toward the Launching Bay. Steven looked at Venussa. 'You could have gone with them.'

'They'll manage without me. And you don't know the Ark like I do. You'll still need me to help you find the bomb.'

Steven nodded gratefully: 'Then let's try behind that central scan.'

Together, they continued with their search.

Number Two came in from the terrace. He was agitated as he addressed his leader: 'Number Four has spoken to others and some more of them have agreed to go with him – including Number Twelve!'

Number One looked up. 'Number Twelve? But he was in charge of the building of the bomb and knows where it is hidden!' He started out, signalling to Number Two and his other supporters to follow him. 'I have changed my mind! We must stop them from returning to the Ark.'

Once they had left, the Doctor addressed Dodo. 'A falling-out among friends!' He grasped the lapels of his jacket thoughtfully. 'Now that could be a dangerous thing . . . or, on the other hand, it could be to our advantage.'

He started to walk out to the terrace to see what was going on, but a Monoid who had stayed behind to watch over them indicated with his weapon that the Doctor should stay indoors.

What the Doctor had been denied seeing was that the progress of Number Four and his party was suddenly intercepted by Number One and the other Monoids who had chosen to follow him.

Number One levelled up his weapon so that it covered Number Four.

'What is the meaning of this?' Number Four demanded. 'We are going back to the Ark, and you have agreed to our decision.'

'I have changed my mind, and it is against my orders that you should be allowed to leave.'

'Your orders! You have given too many and delivered them unwisely. Now they mean nothing to us.'

In reply Number One fired off his weapon. It emitted a flash, and Number Seven was extinguished as he moved forward protectively in front of Number Four. Immediately, Number Four and his companions fired their weapons as they scrambled for cover. In moments, battle had broken out between the two groups of Monoids.

They were evenly matched and fought desperately. The flashes from their weapons, screeching and cracking, echoed throughout the Refusian countryside which, until now, had always known peace.

Monoids were caught in the blasts that left nothing behind except scorches upon the landscape. In a very short time ten ... then fifteen ... then thirty of their number had perished in this way.

Some were luckier than others, managing to scramble away from the area. Among them was Number One, who beat a hasty retreat when he saw the death and destruction that was being visited upon his followers.

As they scrambled away he addressed Number Two: 'Tell me, what happened to Number Twelve?'

'I think he was hit, Number One. But I am not sure. In the confusion I lost track.'

'Then send a special party to guard the Launchers! Whatever happens, Number Twelve must not be allowed to leave because he knows the secrets of the bomb.'

Number Two nodded and turned to instruct others who had followed them. They then left and made their way to the area where the Launchers were parked, while Number Two followed Number One.

Having been denied a view of the events outside the castle, the Doctor and Dodo were trying to put their Monoid captor off guard by playing a game of snakes-and-ladders that they had found in the drawer of a table.

They were succeeding. The Monoid was puzzled and could not work these two strangers out at all. Where others might have protested and tried to challenge him, this man and the young girl seemed to be embroiled in a useless, pointless game.

'One ... two ... three – and up the ladder I go!' Dodo exclaimed.

'H'm!' the Doctor said. 'You seem to have all the luck in this game.'

He threw the dice. It rolled ... and stopped with the five dots showing up.

'Ah!' Dodo exclaimed, and took great delight in moving the Doctor's counter for him. It landed on the head of a snake and she ran down its length to position his piece well behind hers. The Doctor grimaced.

Strange beings, the Monoid thought. Rumour had it that they had not only travelled through space, but time as well. He could not bring himself to believe it. He had a private theory that they were odd descendants of the original Guardians who had managed to hide on the Ark in some out-of-the-way corner. That made more sense. Then his thoughts were interrupted as the Doctor called over: 'Are you sure you won't join us in this game, old chap?'

The Monoid moved over to the table and stared down at the board.

'What is the meaning of this?' he demanded.

'Sorry ... don't follow you!'

'You mock the Monoids with that image.' The Doctor was puzzled, then realised that the Monoid was referring to the snakes that were colourfully drawn on the board. The Monoid continued: 'You go up those ladders and *down* the snakes. It should be the other way round.'

Impatiently he grasped the board and threw it onto the floor.

Dodo pouted. 'Now we'll never know who would have won that game.'

The Doctor observed the Monoid as the creature walked nervously away.

'I think *we* did!' the Doctor said, quietly.

*

Number Twelve and a couple of other Monoids cautiously approached a parked Launcher.

'We must be careful,' Number Twelve advised.

'Yes,' one of the others agreed. 'Tell me, Number Twelve, is it true that you know about the secrets of the bomb?'

'I designed it, I helped build it,' came the reply. 'If we can get back to the Ark I can at least halt the timing mechanism and render the bomb inactive!'

Everything seemed to be quiet as they approached the craft. A last, cautious look around them, and then they scrambled through its doors.

Once inside, Number Twelve operated the lever that closed the door. Then he switched on the power source, and they all relaxed as the Launcher rose into the air.

But on the ground below them a group of the Monoids who had been detailed by Number Two looked up as they saw the Launcher rising.

'Concentrate your fire,' cried one of them. 'We must destroy that machine!'

The flares from their heat weapons hit the Launcher at the same time. There was an explosion . . . and the remains of the devastated Launcher rained down from the sky.

At the same time, not far away, another Launcher was landing on Refusis.

Dassuk operated the door lever. As the door opened Maharis immediately stood up.

'Maharis, where are you going?' Dassuk asked.

'Out!'

'Better make sure that everything is all right first.'

Maharis shook his head impatiently, anxious to set foot on Refusis. He stepped out of the craft. Looking about him, he smiled as he saw a land of apparent peace. Quickly he started walking forward. Then he paused as he saw Number One a short distance away, in company with other Monoids.

Maharis eagerly started toward him, crying out: 'Master! I

am here . . .'

Number One looked up, startled to see him there. Then he coldly aimed his weapon at him. Maharis screamed as the first blast of heat hit him, the scream quickly dying away to nothing.

Dassuk had been watching from the doorway and had seen Number One in the distance. At the same time he could see other Monoids shadowing Number One and his party, and then, as he watched, the two groups engaged in battle.

Dassuk turned to the other Guardians.

'Come!' he said. 'Let's get out of here while the Monoids are fighting each other.'

Hastily, they left the Launcher and started running across fields, seeking the cover of trees and bushes. As they ran Dassuk occasionally caught glimpses of the scattered fighting that was taking place between the Monoids.

Ahead of him, he and the others saw the castle. They ran toward it.

The Doctor, Dodo and the Monoid had seen the flashes of the heat weapons from an open window. The Doctor sensed that the Monoid was disturbed and uneasy.

'What the heck is going on?' Dodo asked.

'It looks like an outbreak of civil war,' the Doctor replied.

'At this rate they'll all kill each other and a lot more besides,' Dodo observed. 'And I don't think the Refusians are going to like that!'

'So you know these beings, the Refusians?' the Monoid asked. 'What are they like? How do they behave?'

'In a way that I don't think you'll appreciate, old chap,' the Doctor replied.

The Monoid looked as though he was going to ask another question . . . but just then Dassuk entered the hall, running in quickly.

'Master!' he panted, addressing the Monoid. 'Number One needs your help out there!'

The Monoid stared at him suspiciously. 'I don't know you,' he said.

'Perhaps that's because I've always worked for Number Fifty-Two,' said Dassuk. 'The Monoid Master who was in charge of the polar regions on the Ark.'

'Oh, that place,' the Monoid replied. 'No wonder I have never seen you – I never went there.' He glanced out of the window. 'You say that Number One has asked for me?'

'Yes.'

'Very well. Meanwhile, keep an eye on these strangers!'

The Monoid left, taking his weapon with him. Dassuk breathed a sigh of relief and turned to face the Doctor.

'What *is* going on out there, Doctor? All that fighting ...'

'Nothing for you to worry about, dear boy ... just local politics!' He studied Dassuk. 'What is more important is this ... is the Ark still all right?'

'So far. But they haven't found the bomb yet.'

'But we now know where it is!' said the Doctor. 'And we must warn them immediately, so come along!'

As the Doctor, Dodo and Dassuk made their way to the area where the Launchers rested, they had to move cautiously through the warring factions of the Monoids. The battle between the two groups had spread far and wide, judging by the number of scorch marks that they found on the earth.

'The way they're going at it there won't be enough left to make a football team,' Dodo whispered. Then they dropped to the ground hastily as a tree ahead suddenly burst into flames. 'Cor ... that was a close one!'

As they crept through a ravine, they heard a moan coming from some bushes surrounding a tree.

'What's that?' Dodo asked.

'It sounds like someone in pain,' the Doctor replied. He went to investigate, then called: 'Come here!'

They joined him and found themselves staring down at an injured Number Four.

'What happened to you?' the Doctor asked the Monoid.

'I was in that tree,' Number Four replied. 'But a branch I was leaning on broke and I fell. I think I've broken my leg.'

The Doctor examined it, remembering the anatomy scan of the Monoids that he had studied on his first visit to the Ark, under the guidance of the microbiologist, Rhos. His fingers moved along the leg, pausing when he found the fracture.

He looked up at the others. 'Get some sticks. We have to make an improvised splint.'

Dassuk stared at him, bewildered. 'But surely you're not suggesting that we help one of his kind?'

'He is a living creature and he is injured – so we must help!' the Doctor stated.

'I'll get the sticks,' Dodo said.

'And we'll need that belt that holds in your tunic,' the Doctor said to Dassuk. 'It doesn't seem to have any purpose other than being decorative.'

Dassuk sighed. He was still not certain of the Doctor's thinking and was disturbed by his concern for a creature that he and the other Guardians had always considered their enemy. But then he took off his belt and passed it to the Doctor.

'Here you are,' he said. 'But by rights it should be used to strangle him!'

'You have a lot to learn,' said the Doctor reprovingly.

Then he concentrated on placing the sticks around the Monoid's leg. Once in place, he bound them firmly with the belt.

The Monoid moaned and winced with pain as the Doctor completed his first aid.

'That will have to do for the moment,' he said. 'When things settle down we'll organise something better for you.'

Number Four was grateful and nodded his head. 'Thank you, Doctor.' He looked at the others. 'And thank you for your help.'

They left him and continued on their way. As they walked Dassuk addressed the Doctor: 'He *thanked* us! ... And what's more, I think he meant it.'

'Now you're beginning to learn something,' the Doctor replied.

As the Doctor and his companions reached the area around the Launcher, they found some straggling remnants of the Monoids still engaged in battle.

More flashes, more Monoids extinguished. Then those who had suffered the greater losses threw aside their weapons and surrendered to their opponents.

One of the victorious party, Number Eighteen, signalled for his friends to cease firing. Then he glanced aside and saw the Doctor.

'Come forward, Doctor. We choose not to be your enemies, but your friends!'

The Doctor and his companions approached cautiously.

'Are you friends of Number Four?' the Doctor asked.

'Yes! We no longer support Number One. We wish to make sure that the Ark survives and that the bomb is rendered harmless.'

'Well, at least I know where it is, so I can inform those aboard the Ark. Meanwhile, Number Four is in that ravine over there. He is injured and requires assistance.'

'Then we will see that he gets it,' replied Number Eighteen. He signalled for the others to follow him, and they started away.

'Let's hurry!' urged the Doctor. 'No time to waste ... we must get our message through!'

He, Dodo and Dassuk entered the Launcher.

Number Eighteen and the others found the injured Number Four. Quickly, they gathered together branches and formed a rough and ready stretcher. They were about to move off, carrying their comrade, when they were challenged by Number One and a group of his supporters.

'Where are you taking him?' Number One demanded.

'To the castle, where there is the chance that he might receive proper treatment,' Number Eighteen replied.

'From the Doctor?'

'No. The Doctor and his friends are on their way back to the Ark.'

Number Eighteen pointed to the distant Launcher as it took off, leaving Refusis behind.

'Then if not by the Doctor, by whom?' Number One demanded. 'The Refusians?'

'Perhaps.'

'You are a traitor!' Number One pronounced. He addressed his supporters. 'Attack them!'

They started firing. There were more casualties, but Number Four was quickly lowered out of sight and Number Eighteen and his companions fought back, using the cover of nearby rocks.

This gave them the advantage. In a short while Number One could see that his group was getting the worst of the exchange and, at his side, Number Two was hit and extinguished.

Number One again fled the field, this time travelling alone. Number Eighteen saw him go and started off in pursuit.

The chase led through the ravine, Number One desperately seeking the cover of scattered rocks on its sides to try and get away. Occasionally he paused and fired back, but Number Eighteen kept coming.

A river coursed through the ravine. Number One plunged into it, gaining the other side. There he continued running, Number Eighteen sniping at him from the other bank.

At the end of the ravine the river tumbled over rocks into a waterfall. Number One paused, seeing a cave on the other side, and, judging that he was far enough ahead of his pursuer, he started scrambling over the rocks to try and reach its safety.

Number Eighteen paused and carefully levelled up the aim of his weapon. A searing flash ... and while the shot did not hit his quarry squarely, it side-swiped him and knocked him off balance.

Number One screamed as he plunged over the lip of the waterfall and his body contorted as it fell into the swirling waters hundreds of feet below.

The Launcher settled back in the bay aboard the Ark and the Doctor, Dodo and Dassuk stepped out to be greeted by Steven and Venussa.

'I'm glad you're back, Doctor,' said Steven. 'We could not make sense of your radio signal. It kept breaking up.'

The Doctor strode quickly ahead, leading them into the Great Hall.

'What I was trying to tell you about was the location of the bomb ...'

'That's the part we couldn't understand. Where is it?'

'It's up there! In the head of the statue!'

They stared up in amazement.

Venussa was dismayed. 'But in that case how are we going to tackle it? The statue is so heavy!'

'You must have some lifting gear!' Steven exclaimed. 'We only need to get it into one of the Launching Bays.'

'Nothing that can handle anything like that!'

'H'm!' the Doctor mused. 'Quite a problem!'

The voice of the Refusian echoed through the Great Hall. 'I think I can help you! But first you must clear the area around the statue.'

'What do we do?' Dassuk asked.

'As he says, dear boy, as he says,' the Doctor said.

Steven, Dassuk and Venussa immediately started moving the Guardians away from the vicinity of the statue. Steven looked up. 'Will that do?' he asked.

'Yes!' came the reply from the Refusian. 'Now leave the rest to me!'

Fascinated, they watched as the statue was suddenly moved on its base, as though grasped by a being of great strength.

'It ... it's moving!' Dodo cried.

'Yes,' said Steven. 'But let's hope that the movement doesn't set the bomb off!'

Steadily the statue was eased away from the position that it had occupied for seven hundred years. It was moved across the Great Hall and into the area of the Launch Bays, and there was set down, ready for expulsion.

'I have done my part,' said the Refusian.

Dodo was awe-struck. Finally she gulped and said, 'Nice one, Charlie!'

'But when you send it away from this spaceship, aim it at the Refusian moon. Like the one near your Earth it is only dust and rock. There is no life on it.'

'We will,' Dassuk replied. He manned the controls of the expulsion panel and then pressed the trigger.

The statue sped out into space, away from the Ark, finally exploding in a mighty but harmless strike against the surface of the Refusian moon.

A message came through from a Launcher on Refusis. 'This is Monoid Number Eighteen. I wish to speak to the Doctor.'

'Yes, Number Eighteen,' the Doctor replied. 'What is it?'

'Everything is under control on the planet Refusis. We have made contact with the Refusians, including one who calls herself Mary, and we are organising the return of the rest of the Launchers to the Ark so that everything aboard it can be brought down here.'

'Thank you,' the Doctor replied. 'Message gratefully received and acknowledged.'

The Doctor broke off contact.

Dodo addressed Dassuk and Venussa. 'Do you think you'll be able to get everything down onto Refusis now?'

'We'll manage,' Venussa replied.

'Especially if the Refusians help us,' Dassuk added.

The voice of the Refusian said, 'We'll do everything we

can! Everything to assist you in settling on our planet.'

'Thank you,' Dassuk said.

'But one thing you must do ...'

'What's that?' Venussa asked.

'Make peace with the Monoids. A lasting, far-seeing and constructive peace!'

'He's right!' the Doctor observed. 'A long time ago your ancestors accepted responsibility for the welfare of the Monoids. But they were treated as servants – almost as slaves – so that it was no wonder that, when they got the chance, they repaid you in kind.'

'Unless you learn to live together there is no future for you on Refusis,' the voice continued.

Dassuk considered the proposal, then nodded. 'We understand ... and we agree!'

The Doctor patted him on the shoulder. 'Well said, my boy. You have started to learn well.' He turned to the others. 'You know, you must live with understanding as well as hope. H'm ... I once said that to one of your ancestors a long time ago!'

The Doctor, Dodo and Steven stood by for some time, observing with interest the mass landings from the Ark onto the surface of Refusis.

True to their word, the Monoids, led by Number Eighteen, had returned to the spaceship with the Launchers. They then set to with a will, co-operating in the loading of the craft with the multitude of storage trays containing the Earth's life.

These, and the Re-enhancing Incubators that would give the microcell organisms their original shape and form, were taken to points on the planet that the Refusians suggested.

The operation became a model of efficient organisation, each of the Guardians and Monoids having an allotted task and following it faithfully. The Doctor realised that the Main Edicts of the long voyage were coming to fulfilment, and knew that there was something else that he had to see.

141

He addressed Dassuk and Venussa: 'With your permission I would like to make one further trip to Refusis in order to meet some of your ancestors.'

'Of course, Doctor!' came the reply. 'And you, too, Steven and Dodo.'

So the trip was arranged and once more they descended on the surface of the planet. There, Dassuk and Venussa accompanied them in a conveyor to a large hall that had been taken over for the special purposes of Re-enhancement.

The machines stood in a row; glass-fronted cubicles that were manned by Guardians and Monoid specialists.

As the Doctor and his companions watched, trays were placed in them. There was an intensity of bright light, and moments later the doors of the cubicles were opened and out walked human beings, Monoids and all the other forms of life that had made the journey.

After their long, suspended sleep they blinked for a moment, then moved off to take their place among the rapidly expanding population of the planet.

One of them, a young Guardian, looked at the Doctor. He asked: 'This is Refusis?'

'Yes.'

The young man sighed with relief. 'Thank heavens – we've made it, despite my mistake.'

'Oh, what was that?'

'I opened some valves in the wrong way aboard the spaceship.'

'H'm! It doesn't seem to have made any difference,' the Doctor said reassuringly. 'What is your name?'

'Niash,' the young man replied. 'I travelled in the time of the First Commander ... and his daughter, Mellium!'

'Ah, yes,' the Doctor replied softly, glancing at Steven and Dodo. 'But now, Niash, go and live your life to the full, as you were intended to.'

Niash nodded and walked out of the hall.

*

Back aboard the Ark the Doctor, Dodo and Steven turned to Venussa and Dassuk.

'Time for us to go!' the Doctor said. 'Goodbye!'

There was a general exchange of goodbyes between them all, and then the Doctor and his companions were driven out into the jungle aboard a conveyor.

Venussa watched them go.

'Do you think we'll ever see them again?' she asked Dassuk.

'Perhaps,' he replied. 'Or if we don't, our children might.' He reflected. 'Or our children's children.'

'If we were to tell them the story do you think they'd believe us? Or would they just dismiss it as a legend?'

Dassuk looked at her firmly.

'We'll make them believe it!'

The machinery within the TARDIS whined, whirred and clanked ... and within seconds it disappeared from the glade in the jungle where it had been resting.

Inside, the Doctor was busy adjusting his flight controls. He jiggled a lever and when this action produced no results he gave the machine a kick.

'Ah, that's it!' he said with satisfaction. 'Now the Gravitational Bearing is working at full strength!'

'Oh, I'm glad to hear that!' Dodo said. 'It makes me feel OK when that flipping lot is behaving itself!'

'Yes,' the Doctor mused. 'And now that we're under way I think it is about time that we did something about that English of yours! Now let me see ... I know! Say the following after me: "The rain in Spain falls mainly on the plain."'

'Like heck it does,' Dodo retorted. 'The last time I was there, it bucketed down!'

The Doctor sighed, recognising that he had a mammoth task in front of him. Then he glanced at Steven as the latter asked, 'Where are we going now, Doctor?'

'Yes, where?' Dodo echoed.

'You know better than to ask something like that!' the Doctor replied. 'I – and TARDIS – can promise you a journey, but ...'

'What?' they asked in unison.

'... no guaranteed destination!'